# TO LOVE, HONOUR AND OBEY

## *The Yorkshire Saga Series Book One*

### Valerie Holmes

SAPERE
BOOKS

# TO LOVE, HONOUR AND OBEY

Published by Sapere Books.

20 Windermere Drive, Leeds, England, LS17 7UZ,
United Kingdom

**saperebooks.com**

ISBN: 978-1-912786-41-1

# Prologue

Joshua dismounted and stared through the heavy mist at the outline of the low cruck built cottage. On such a night, shadows moved and the cold fear within him grew. He was not a man to be unnerved easily, but six months of undercover work hung on the success of this meeting. One name, a traitor to the Crown was all he needed — just a name.

He paused, trying to shrug off an unfamiliar feeling — a nagging doubt, which had crept into his mind and would not give him any peace. Joshua tied the animal's reins to a cart by the side of the deserted building. Darkness was falling like a sodden cloak over the surrounding moorland. The cold seeped through to his bones from a growing unease that gnawed at his gut. Joshua was not a superstitious man, but tonight, in this desolate place, he had never felt so alone. Shrugging the feeling away, he cautiously approached the old cottage door.

No flickering light from the small window greeted him from within. Once the name was revealed, his mission was finished; then he would return south to his family.

Joshua raised his cavalryman's boot and kicked the door open; it creaked as it swung wide over the muddied flagstones. He was on the brink of breaking a whole ring of free traders and catching the scum who would sell information on his own country to the French.

The door rebounded; he stood forward in its wake. The familiar voice greeted him from the depths.

"Josh, I've been waiting here for thee, wondering if you'd lost your way, man." Oberon Spratt's words cut sharply through the air, along with his stink and the smoke from his clay pipe.

Joshua edged inside, his eyes slowly adjusting to the gloom. "I told you that I'd come. I keep my word, Spratt." He made out the shape of the tall, wiry frame standing a few feet in front of him, topped by the outline of a battered tricorn hat.

"Aye, so you did. It's about time we had this meeting, Josh. It's long overdue." He slowly dragged on his pipe, releasing the smoke back into the air, seemingly savouring the moment.

"Overdue?" Joshua repeated, peering into the shadows. "It was arranged only two days since." There was something about the wretch's tone which made Joshua wary. "Where is the man, Spratt? I've travelled half the night. I told you clearly what the deal could be worth. You've seen the bonds. I want what he has to sell, and I will only bargain with the king … not his minion. If you're wasting my time, I'll go elsewhere... My contacts are becoming impatient." He took a step away toward the door.

A flash of light illuminated the room as Spratt flicked a spark toward a lamp's wick. Joshua watched it jump into life. The shutters on the cottage window were closed; gaps were breached with old sacking.

"Don't be hasty, Josh. I told you the man was interested, but we do things our way or should I say … his. Bonds may be good, but we prefer to deal in gold or coin." His mouth curled into an uneven smile, displaying teeth that were not all his own; the eyes remained hard, black as Whitby jet.

Joshua waited.

Spratt gestured for him to come closer. "You wanted to meet the man at the top. Well 'his lordship', or should I calls him 'king' if you prefer, don't want to travel to these parts to see strangers at their whim, he only comes to the one he trusts — me good self, Mr Oberon Spratt. So you're out of luck. Some calls him a traitor, see; I call him a man of business — his own. He will see you, though, don't doubt it." He winked at Joshua. He was obviously enjoying toying with him. "I have a name written down for you, all pretty see, so you can read it clearly. Then you can become better acquainted." His grin broadened as he tossed something onto the table: a piece of parchment, folded in two. It fell by the side of the flickering lamp; quickly he pinned it down firmly with one tobacco-stained finger.

Joshua did not trust this man any more than he would have the wretch's dead father, Abel Solomon Spratt, an infamous smuggler who happily murdered any who stood in his way. He was from Joshua's home county of Kent. Yet both father and son had attained powerful positions in their lifetimes. Oberon owned boats, purchased from the profits of the trade. Both men had known power, just as the fine land-owning gentry did. Only the Spratts' power belonged to an underworld in which no true gentleman should ever belong.

"Waste no more of my time. Give me his name and tell me where I can find him!" Joshua stepped forward.

Spratt quickly held the paper near the lamp's flame.

"Then you will have your preferred coin," Joshua added quickly.

"Not so eager." Spratt played with the note, balancing it within his fingers. "You know, Josh, my father was a decent man." Spratt stared pointedly at him.

Joshua's eyes were fixed on the paper. He did not appreciate Spratt's nostalgic outburst. "A father should be, in the eyes of his son at least."

"Maybe not in the eyes of the authorities, eh, Josh? Abel looked after his family and friends damned well. We cared for our own down there just like I oversee folks up here. He was murdered when I had just turned fourteen." Spratt's face looked hard and unyielding. "I watched with the crowd as his life was jerked out of his body; I could not help him, Josh. It wasn't clean and I had to watch… That hurt."

Joshua sensed Spratt's festering anger. "You have my condolences. Now, give me the man's name," he persisted.

"You have sons, Josh, don't you?" Spratt continued, ignoring his demands, slowly turning the paper over and over between his fingers … tantalisingly near the naked flame.

Joshua could feel the abyss growing closer, or rather, felt as if he were being drawn toward it. He had to grab the note and flee.

Spratt threw the paper at him. "Here, take it! Look and read that name. Etch it on your heart, man, the name of a traitor!"

Joshua snatched it, opening it so that the light made it legible. His forehead creased in disbelief as he read the familiar surname scribbled upon it: his own. "What is the meaning of this?" he shouted, his hand reaching for his pistol. His identity! The abyss beckoned. Too late, he stared straight down the barrel of a Ketland flintlock pistol.

Spratt was smiling. "Your sons are how old? Seventeen, the youngest, isn't it?"

Joshua realised how many of the previous months he had spent in a secret gloom, much of it in hovels such as this with the likes of Oberon Spratt. Soon the authorities should have secured the traitor whilst he returned to his family to celebrate the turn of another century. He needed to keep his wits on Spratt's sly eyes.

"You sent my father to the gallows. They judged him ill, like I shall you, Joshua Rossington. I stand here in judgement and I say you're guilty of taking a life. 'Thou shalt not kill!' That's what the good book says, isn't it? So who is the traitor now? You said you wanted to be one of us ... well we don't trust strangers so readily, see. Funny how history repeats itself, isn't it, Josh? They'll miss you, them sons of yours." Spratt was smiling. "I'm going to avenge my father's death at last."

"You're mad, Spratt! He was caught; he was a smuggler and a murderer who knew the risks. I can pay you much more than you take here. If you know my real name, you must know my connections. Spare my life and I'll set you up somewhere safe — just name your price!" Joshua saw a hint of temptation in Spratt's eyes. He seized his moment, ducking and grabbing a three legged stool. He swung it wildly at the man's gun. There was a flash as a shot rang out; both narrowly missed being burnt as the deafening noise exploded to the side of them. Rolling across the table, Joshua crashed onto the stone floor; Spratt followed, his hat toppling onto the ground next to them. Like animals they set upon one another, each trying to land a deadly blow. Spratt dug his nails into Joshua's neck with one hand, swinging at him with the other. Joshua felt the sting of his flesh as his skin tore, a trickle of blood drawn before Joshua threw Spratt over his head. He sprang up ready to land a final crashing blow into the man's jaw. Relief flooded though him as his instincts had played him false; he would survive this night.

Another pistol shot ripped into the cottage, the dazzling flare and sudden crack of noise stopping him mid punch, but it wasn't from Spratt's or Joshua's. Both men separated, diving for cover as they sought the origin of the bullet. A cloaked figure filled the doorway.

The figure stepped forward and prodded Joshua's prone torso with the toe of his muddied boot. Spratt was tossed a weighty purse. He caught it in one hand.

"You know what to do with him?"

Spratt nodded. "Aye, Throw him off Stangcliffe," he said simply, as he replaced his tricorn upon his head, carefully tilting it slightly to the right.

He nodded back. "Good. It is a sad, but necessary act we commit this day, my friend. Torch the building when it is done; leave no traces of him being here. He has powerful family and friends." The man gave a crooked smile then left, remounting his horse, riding away into the distance.

Spratt stared at the departing figure as he merged into the mist like a demon of the night, then placed his pipe carefully back in his pocket and stared down at Joshua. A broad grin spread across his narrow lips. "You're wrong, 'Your Majesty', this is not a sad act, but it's one that is long overdue."

Joshua regained a blurred consciousness as his world jolted along, shaking his aching body. He soon realised that he was in the back of a conveyance. His first thought — escape! His legs felt useless. Joshua tried to sit up, but he could not find his balance. His head throbbed from the shock of the blow and the perpetual motion of the vehicle as it jarred over many ruts. In desperation he fumbled for a pencil from his pocket, then his wallet from his greatcoat pocket and scratched what he hoped would be a legible message on the back of the piece of paper he had sketched on earlier. Joshua was a traitor in the eyes of this gang. By their law, he was also a condemned man.

Joshua could not focus clearly; he had to scribble by feel. Just a few words ... anything, just in case he was found ... just in case... He hoped the marks made were legible. Struggling, he tried to wrap it up safely and replace it within the hidden pocket of his greatcoat. He prayed for clarity of vision. A piercing pain shot through his head as the wagon traversed another rut, but it was nothing to the one that shot through his heart when he recalled seeing the man in the doorway — he had been hopelessly betrayed.

The jolting finally stopped. With gargantuan effort, he forced himself up onto his elbows, rolling to the end of the cart. His body stopped against the tail board, but his head still spun. The flap was lowered and Joshua felt a hand grab his collar and drag him out, landing on rough wet ground. The wind was strong and the sound of breaking waves seemed to echo within his thumping head. Using all his remaining strength, he tried to stand, to place one foot in front of the other, his senses befuddled.

Through blurred vision, he tried to see the face; the wiry figure took shape, one hand helping Joshua steady himself as he struggled to his feet. The wind threatened to blow him off balance again, but Spratt was stronger than he looked.

Salvation was upmost in Joshua's mind. "I can make you rich, Spratt, just think — anything you wanted, or any woman you craved. You could have what you truly desire — anything." Joshua tried to see the blackguard's face clearly. Almost there, he thought, just a few moments more and perhaps he would be able to escape, as his sight slowly began to return. His senses would soon be with him again. Joshua needed time, he needed those vital seconds, just a little more, but time, like his luck, had run out. He grabbed at Spratt's sleeve.

Spratt wasn't interested. "Look down, Josh, and tell me what you see." Spratt pointed to the ground.

Joshua stared at his feet, then he looked a foot or so away, and his grip on Spratt's sleeve tightened with desperation. The man's hand covered his own. "We're on Stangcliffe, the headland!" Joshua exclaimed, as realisation hit him harder than that of the force of the wind. He was inches away from a sheer drop to the sea below where sharp edged rocks hid under each of the crashing waves.

"That's right, Josh. I already have what I truly want — your life. Say hello to my father for me, and, one day, I'll say hello to your son for you!" With one swift move, he yanked Joshua's hand from his coat, spun him around, pushing him hard in the back. "This, Joshua, *is* my heart's desire."

Joshua fell, swept away with the wind. His scream rose as he fell, crashing into the sea below. One word had escaped his lips as he tumbled, dispersing into the air as his final breath, "Willoughby!" A huge wave broke against his body, and the sea claimed its latest victim.

Joshua had gambled everything and lost; the brink of success had led him into the abyss of failure. The traitorous ring had triumphed. They had won.

He hit the rocks.

# Chapter 1

*1805, North Riding, Yorkshire*

Willoughby Rossington gulped the much needed ale down his dry throat, sighed with relief and placed the pewter tankard on the upturned barrel, which doubled as a table. It had been a difficult mission and a hard ride, but Willoughby had managed to flush out his prey, a highwayman, and after a chase across exposed moorland had relieved the country of one more specimen of murdering vermin. Now, he leaned patiently back on the settle, which lined the alcove next to the rear door of the inn, watching for the York coach to arrive.

Discreetly, Willoughby checked the shallow cut on his wrist. It had not been deep enough to sever the vein. Taking a clean strip of linen from a side pocket of his case, he tied it around his wrist as best as he could, using his free hand and teeth. This was not the first time he had been wounded. A pistol shot had caught him as he was chased across a French beach the previous summer. Fortunately, he had not been on his own and was tossed into the bottom of a fishing boat waiting to return him to England. His uncle had called it his initiation — a rite of passage. The slight scar above his left ear would apparently serve to remind him to take greater care. He slipped his wrist inside his cuff and smiled — no more scars, he thought.

A flurry of activity broke out in the yard.

"York coach!" A horn was heard as the vehicle approached.

Willoughby drained the tankard, ran a hand through his fair hair before replacing his hat, picked up his bag and headed out.

He was anxious to be on his way again. The coach had made good time and was busy. A family with two young girls filled most of the inside, so it was with some relief that Willoughby found himself climbing on top. He settled as comfortably as he could, holding on firmly as the horses pulled their burden back out onto the open road, increasing in speed and momentum. Willoughby felt the invitation to attend his uncle, Lord Nathaniel Rossington, in his pocket and relaxed into the journey. The rush of air on his face made him smile. He anticipated his uncle's next set of orders and relished the prospect of serving his country further.

The coach sped between the open moors and fields, slowing as it approached the ancient city of York. Willoughby was aware of the noise emanating from the lunatic asylum as they passed by. He swallowed, feeling pity for the poor souls trapped inside. That would be hell on earth to him, to be trapped like a caged animal, or worse, chained like a bear, perpetually baited.

The vehicle entered through the ancient stone archway and slowed to navigate the heavily soiled mire, making the going heavy as it passed through one of the ancient crumbling Barrs, ready to traverse the narrow lanes inside the old walls, where a mixture of wooden medieval homes with their jutted fronts gave way to the fashionable new stone buildings.

Willoughby looked on in wonder at the might of The Minster, the magnificent cathedral that dominated the cobbled together collections of buildings around it. No matter how often he saw it, he was always impressed. York was a place which confused and delighted his senses by turn. Contrasts were everywhere: putrid stench mingled with the more pleasant aromas of the market, rich living alongside the impoverished.

The coach came to a lumbering halt in front of an old inn. A sign swung dubiously above the door of a phoenix rising from the ashes. It was a sorry depiction of what should have been a lovely image, buffeted by the wind and heavy rain.

The innkeeper rushed around the corner and greeted his new arrivals, despite the pouring rain. All was a hive of activity. A small step was brought for the passengers to climb down onto. Willoughby knew that Lord Rossington would have been informed that the coach was in. He would be expected to report shortly but he was tempted to go inside and warm and dry himself.

Beth heard the excitement as word reached the inn that the coach was approaching. She had been preparing food in the back in readiness. In her dreams, she would get on the coach, dressed smartly in a travelling coat and be taken to some grand house where her husband or, more likely, her lover, would be awaiting her return. She put down her bread knife at the side of the stone sink, brushed her hands against her coarse skirts and glanced anxiously around her. Dotty, the cook, had gone into the back yard and Irwin Wilkes had left earlier on 'business'. He would normally greet his guests and then return inside — to her. She grabbed her old shawl and pulled it around her shoulders, thinking that he must have been delayed.

Beth knew if she was caught shirking, she would be in for trouble, yet the yearning inside her made her desperate to see who the coach had brought in. The longing to escape the inn, her hellhole, was growing daily. She had nothing of her own and no one to go to, but the coaches came and went and each time her heart desired to go too. She was the bird lost in the ashes and she would take flight, unlike the bird that was trapped on a piece of wood swinging above the doorway.

She ran her fingers through her rich auburn hair, its fiery colour subdued by the need of a wash, though she kept it in relatively good order as she hated the knots. Beth peeped through the serving hatch just to make sure that Irwin Wilkes had not become distracted by his friends and was sitting on his favourite settle. No, he was hovering somewhere outside in his coat. He owned the inn and, although it hurt Beth to think it, he also owned her. Two seasons ago she had been bought by coin from the orphanage where she had grown up as a young woman to serve drinks at the inn. She had no say in the matter, no rights, and was told to be grateful her fate was not a worse one. It was go with Wilkes or live on the filthy streets.

Peering through the musty, smoke-filled tap room she could see the passengers alight from the coach. One man stood alone and slightly to the side. Beth watched him. He did not look as if he intended to enter, she noted with disappointment, but stood surveying the city. He was tall and from what she could see of his features, between high collar and tall hat, handsome. He looked to the inn, but despite the soaking he had had, he decided to move off.

He must be lost, Beth reasoned, so she straightened her shoulders and stepped forward, ready to cross the room and welcome the guests and offer the stranger her help before he decided to leave — if she could. There was something about him that drew her to him. He would fit the image of the man in her daydream well enough. Even though he was clearly a gentleman, she thought, a girl can dream, can't she?

"Beth!"

She froze. Wilkes's footsteps neared as his boots sounded upon the flagstone floor behind her. The weather must have dampened his enthusiasm for being a good host.

"Where d'you think you are off to, my girl?"

She could smell his musk. He spun her around, whipping the worn fabric from her shoulders. The word 'my' resonated in her head as the usual feelings of disgust stirred within her belly. He threw his coat onto a stool.

"Nowhere, Mr Wilkes. I was just a bit cold and I heard all the noise." She tried to keep her voice calm as getting flustered only provoked his temper further. Her eyes were downcast; he took it as a sign of submission. She used it to shield the hatred that burned within them.

"Cold, eh," he repeated, and chuckled. "Go on up to me room. I'll be there shortly." He slapped her rump as she stepped away.

Beth tried not to show him fear or her anger. She picked up her shawl; moth-bitten it may be, but it was hers, and then climbed the wooden steps to his room above, cursing her stupidity and dreading his idea of giving her warmth.

Willoughby stretched to his full height. He was tired, his wrist was sore, but he needed to see his uncle — then he could think about resting before setting off again on his next mission. He was in the north; he was so near to where his father had been murdered. Willoughby's heart desired one mission more than any other: to investigate that 'accident'. No one had been brought to justice. Five years later and he had proved to his uncle he could wheedle out vermin and be trusted, so why not now avenge his father's death?

He approached the grand façade of the elegant terraced house. Willoughby had to stay level-headed; displays of emotion were not appreciated — 'anger was to be challenged into action, not allowed to burn and destroy internally'. His uncle was full of such pearls of wisdom.

He lifted the brass knocker, then crashed it against the door and waited until a liveried servant opened it to him.

"Is my uncle at home?" Willoughby asked.

"Your uncle? May I have your card, sir?" The man spoke stiffly and held out a gloved hand.

Willoughby wondered if he was one of his uncle's agents or just a household servant; either way, he acted like a pompous fool. Willoughby pulled the invitation from his pocket, returning it to its sender. It was his pass to a very different world — one in which he thrived. The man responded with a cursory look up and down as rain dripped off Willoughby's greatcoat and onto the doorstep of the elegant house.

Willoughby met the man's stare in challenge and made to step forward. It had been an uncomfortable journey and his patience was becoming worn. The servant closed the door on him, disappearing with the letter. Willoughby balled his fist and looked across the sodden road, waiting patiently, albeit reluctantly, to be allowed entry. A few minutes later the door reopened.

"My apologies, sir." The man bowed low as he stepped back, allowing Willoughby to pass by him, whilst taking his hat and coat. "This way, if you please, sir."

Willoughby followed him across a chequered floor and down a narrow corridor to a set of doors towards the back of the house. Beyond them was his uncle's study. Immediately Willoughby entered, the doors were shut securely behind him, not one, but two sets separated by a good thick curved wall. This was a necessity, as his uncle could not afford to have his private discussions overheard by anyone.

Willoughby was surprised that the normally officious man was not sitting and looking imposingly at him from behind the large mahogany desk as was his habit. Instead, he stood silently gazing at a painting that adorned the wall above the marble fireplace. Immaculately dressed in a perfectly fitted black coat which accentuated his straight and noble posture, he held his hands clasped behind his back. "Do you know what this is, Willoughby?"

Willoughby sighed. Never a warm word of welcome, but he knew how to respond. "It is a seascape, Uncle." Willoughby stared at it emotionless, almost mimicking his uncle's dour manner until he saw a flash of annoyance showing in the older man's eyes. "A stormy sea and a rescue boat being hauled into the water by the local villagers." Willoughby admired the movement and energy within the painting. One could almost feel the tempest raging and the desperation of the people to launch the life-saving boat into the water.

"What else can you see? Where do you think it is set?" his uncle persisted, staring at him, waiting for Willoughby to look beyond the obvious. It was like a game, a grooming, which both his uncle and his father had played with him since he had been a child.

Willoughby stepped forward, relaxing his pose. He looked at every feature of the painting: the group of people at the water's edge, the windmill behind a row of small fishermen's houses, the firm flat sands, the high rugged headland in the distance and the menacing sea. "By the attire of the people and the geographical features of the land, I would say this is a fishing village on the remote north-east coast." Willoughby glanced at his uncle, waiting for acknowledgement or approval.

"And what reasoning is behind this decision, Willoughby? Have you proof of a logical nature or is this just a wild guess — no more than a lucky whim?"

"No, Uncle, it is not a guess. The boats in the background are the cobles of the Yorkshire design. They land on the flat sandy beaches, cutting through the breakers. The sea is treacherously turbulent and that area is infamous for its wrecks. To the right are the ancient marshlands and dunes, whilst to the left, the steep jutting headland forms a dramatic feature. The boat is one of the new designs of 'lifeboat', which I believe has to be pulled manually down to the beach by the villagers in order to launch it successfully."

His uncle released his hands, relaxing his stance and patted Willoughby firmly on his shoulder. "Excellent observations, Willoughby; you show some intelligence. I'm glad your time at Cambridge was not wasted; you have at least learnt to deduce. So tell me, why am I showing you this merciless place?" Nathaniel Rossington flicked the tails of his coat up into the air and rested against his desk.

"You wish me to go there, no doubt still wearing the robes of a priest and save the poor from the endless toil of their lives and their mortal souls from hell itself, Uncle?" Willoughby raised a cynical brow, as he knew Nathaniel was a sceptical man, a non-believer, a fact he kept very much to the closest family members to avoid unnecessary problems within the society with which he mixed.

"I would say they are beyond salvation and, personally, I should let them rot away within their own grimy existence."

Willoughby was not surprised by the man's sentiment, he had his sights set on saving a nation, apparently forgetting at times that the word represented common men eking out a 'grimy existence' and not just the land itself.

"However, I would also remind you that this is not a game anymore, Willoughby. It is as serious as life and death … yours included." Nathaniel looked at Willoughby, whose gaze did not waver despite his uncle's powerful withering stare. However,

Willoughby did note the fleeting glint of amusement in the man's eyes — a rare sight.

"There are treacherous men earning a lot of money in the region — corruption throughout and within the villages which has spread to the normally decent social strata. I need you in there." He pointed to the painting, his manner intense. "Yes, don your priest's garb and start preaching and listening to as many confessions as you can…"

"Uncle, I am not a priest. I have chosen a very different path now." Willoughby spoke out defiantly, then instantly wished he had controlled his tongue. "Surely, I have proven to you that I would have been wasted in such a role when I refused to follow the path which was laid out for me by Uncle Jeremiah, God rest his soul. I would be better serving as a soldier — please, sir, allow me to hunt down Father's murderers or obtain me a commission so that I may serve, with your blessing."

"I am fully aware of what you are and what you are not. Unless you wish me to return you to 'your initial path' and insist that you are to be permanently planted in a respectable parish with a fat wife and several noisy brats to feed, you would do well to remember how much I do know about you, Willoughby James Rossington!" Nathaniel's words were harsh, but as always, controlled. "You serve best where I place you. Your brother serves the King, you fight a very different battle and I need you here to do it!"

Willoughby nodded, annoyed that this man who had acted as a father to him when his own died prematurely always placed his duty first. More disastrous news had followed the next year when his elder uncle, Jeremiah, had perished in a riding accident. Nathaniel was totally devoted towards his King and country. He buried his pain deeply, though, Willoughby realised. Willoughby had been sent to many a dark place concerning his clandestine role. It had shown him a world very different from the old clubs of St James Street in London and the halls of Cambridge. Nathaniel was a man who demanded and expected nothing less than total obedience from those who served him, whether relative or not, and that had earned him Willoughby's absolute respect.

Willoughby did not want to don the garb of the priesthood. He had his own faith, but preaching was something he found no comfort in. It irked him that he had been made to hide within the role in order to be of some use to his uncle. He should have been the soldier — Charles wanted to stay on the estate, but the uncles had insisted he fought for the family honour, leaving Willoughby's path clear for the priesthood.

"You will win the hearts of one or two of the local people. Use your stealth, wit and common sense, but, Willoughby, remember this is no fool's errand. We have reason to believe that the rot that has set in this area is deep and complex. Every one living there is as guilty as their neighbour of plying the trade. They will not break their ungodly ranks and speak out... Strangers are like foreigners to them, they live in greed and ignorance. Only last month, a riding officer nearly had what brains he possessed spilt from a broken skull after he came across a group of 'fishermen' moving a catch. It was not crabs they had plucked from the sea. The fool shouted warning before shooting!" Nathaniel shook his head. "You have two names to keep in your mind, and I demand that you make your initial contact with them as a priest, someone people will pass by, seeing the uniform and not the man, yet, hopefully, show respect and trust."

Willoughby was surprised by the severity of the tone in his uncle's orders.

"Go to Major Walter Husk, who has a temporary barracks in Whitby. He will brief you on the known smuggling activity along the coast north of Whitby, and then to Reverend Artemis Burdon of St Aidan's at Ebton. He will take you in and give you a base from which to work. I do not want you to use the name 'Rossington'. Our family name will be kept out of this. You travel as Reverend Mr Willoughby James. Make sure you conjure up a credible past-life, which does not link you back to the family or me. You are working incognito. Only Husk and Burdon will know the truth. Both are loyal to the Crown and…"

"My father's murderers…" Willoughby's face was instantly animated. It was on Ebton beach that the body of his father, Joshua, had been washed up. "Is it possible that Father's murderers still walk free after nearly six years?" Each time Willoughby had requested to investigate it he had been turned away with other missions to attend to, keeping him far away from this part of the country. It was always with the promise that when the time was right, his turn would come. Now he needed to know if that time was here. Willoughby clenched his fists at his side as the years of frustration and training mixed with his eagerness to set off on his own personal quest grew.

"Of course it is possible, Willoughby!" Nathaniel stood tall and looked into Willoughby's deep brown eyes as if analysing his private thoughts. "You need to put all personal issues aside. We both do. We are working for our country, for the very survival of our nation." Nathaniel swallowed as if struggling to keep his composure. "We are at war with the French. The trade forgets its loyalties and anything is sold for the right price. If, and I mean *if*, there is a link between my brother's early demise and the current tenuous situation, then I expect you to discover it and act accordingly. They went to ground, but have now risen stronger than ever. But remember this: King and country first, revenge last! Do I make myself clear?"

Nathaniel raised his eyebrows.

"Yes, sir!"

"Oh, and one more thing to remember: the harbinger of evil can be both male or female. Your father was engaging in an affair as well as his 'work'. It may have been the cause of his downfall."

Willoughby's attention had wandered to the painting, straining at the menacing sea and the headland beyond. He swallowed, for it must have been a cold and lonely death to die in those waters alone. At the mention of an affair, so calmly announced, Willoughby's head shot back around to look at his uncle.

"Affair? With who?"

"I do not know who. You will not fall into the same trap, will you, my young priest?"

Willoughby was taken aback. He had never thought it possible that his father had had an affair, for his mother had died of a broken heart four years since.

Nathaniel patted him on the back firmly.

"Here is a purse. The sooner you go and pay your respects to your aunt, the sooner I shall have peace from her on this matter. I swear the woman can hear through the walls of a fortress. May your God be with you, and I hope you come back to us safely from this vipers' nest, Willoughby."

# Chapter 2

Willoughby slipped into the library and changed back into the uniform he had been instructed to wear. His high spirits slipped away as he thought about his father. He had missed him for most of his life. When he was there, they spent as much time together as they could, but the partings were hard. Willoughby still winced inside when he recalled the morning Nathaniel summoned him into his office to break the news that the man he idolised would never return again. The grief he still felt was packed down inside him by controlled anger. He would find the murderer and...

"Willoughby!" his aunt's voice summoned.

He saw the worry on the woman's face as he entered the day room. Without a word, he bent forward and kissed her forehead gently under her lace bonnet; the aroma of lavender oil surrounded her.

"Willoughby, you disappoint me. You could have finished your studies and lived in a quiet parish at home; Hythe perhaps?" The lady placed her hand on Willoughby's and smiled at her nephew. She was sitting by the window of the large room, reminiscent of the beauty of Rossington Hall, their family home.

"No, Aunt Eliza, I must go where I am called. I may have disappointed you, but I am still able to help the cause..." He stumbled, he could lie to anyone when he needed to, but this dear lady knew him too well. "There is much hardship and need for spiritual growth in the north. I have to find my own path to my calling..."

"Don't patronise me as if I am a senile old woman! You are a waste of a good man." She straightened her back. "Why could you not be content to be the Reverend Willoughby James Rossington? When you were advised to join the church..."

"Told to, Aunt," he corrected.

"You did not obey Jeremiah's wishes though, did you?"

"My path was being forced upon me," he said bluntly. "My wish was to join the army."

"Don't change the subject, Willoughby. Your Uncle Jeremiah had your safety and wellbeing in mind, bless his soul; we had already lost your dear father. Why could you not accept a normal parish life, settle down with some pleasant girl and have —"

"An incredibly dull life, no doubt!" Willoughby added.

"You really are developing a very bad habit of interrupting your elders. It just will not do!" She stared at him and waited for his response; an apology was expected.

"I forget my manners. You were saying?" Willoughby smiled at her to appease her sense of propriety.

"And have a very satisfying and rewarding existence, is what I was about to say!" She stared pointedly at him, tilting her head to elevate her nose slightly. "Your uncle has influence; you could have had the pick of the best parish our beautiful country could offer. Why go to such a cold place as the northeast coast?"

"Your hearing is exceptional, Aunt," Willoughby commented dryly, wondering how she managed to know so much of his and Nathaniel's private plans.

The lady stared at him refusing to be side-tracked. "I have lived with your uncle for many years, Willoughby."

"My dear Aunt, I seek to live my life, and not merely exist within it, whilst watching others living theirs as they choose to." Willoughby looked at her hoping for a glimmer of understanding.

"Do you think for one moment that the peasant farmer has a choice in the way he lives? Is everyone else so fortunate as to have a choice other than you, sir? Do women have any choice at all, regarding their lot in this world? We are people too!" She was flustered, her lace bonnet flicked in the air as her head bobbed around as she snapped out her words. "Does every maid fall in love and choose her own husband? I think not!"

"No, Aunt, I don't think or presume that."

"Then, my dear Willoughby, why should you be any different to the rest of us mere mortals? You, like everyone else, have your duty to do." She calmed herself.

Willoughby sighed. It was easier to argue with a man of law than with this sharp- witted woman.

"So tell me, how did you acquire that fresh wound on your wrist?" She raised an eyebrow. "From the edge of a sword, I should wager."

"You should not wager on anything, Aunt. However, your sight is still very astute." Willoughby looked into her pale blue eyes. "I was doing God's work."

"Poppycock! You work for your Uncle Nathaniel, and don't try to deny it!" She tilted her head back further to look up at him. Accusingly, her eyes met his.

"Uncle works for his earthly king. I work for our heavenly one." He watched as his aunt's face flushed with annoyance and exasperation.

"I know how many hats my husband has and I also know he would share them with you, too. I have been a widow of your uncle's government office all my married life. He cares not for the expendable when King and country are perceived to be at risk. Your father was a good man; like you, he was a man of honour." Her eyes glistened with moisture as she spoke. "If Joshua had lived, you would never have been allowed to fritter your life away on foolish missions!"

"Aunt Eliza, if he had lived, I would be fighting Napoleon's army because father would, like I do, believe we should each do our duty. I am still doing it. You cannot deny me that right. No one can rest easy until Bonaparte is defeated and peace resumes once more. Evil has to be met head on; you cannot hide from it. I also understand Father was a good man and his death was a tragedy…"

"It was murder and you, my boy, know it only too well!" She stared at him, but this time her eyes were softer, pleading. "You are wrong. He would have wanted you to be safe. I've watched the anger in you grow these last few years, since you discovered a little about the circumstances of Joshua's death. Are you determined to follow this folly through?"

"Aunt, you should not worry yourself so. Our lives are in God's hands, not ours. No one can determine our future, but Him."

"What! If I should not worry, pray tell me who should? You preach very well, for one who denies his true calling!"

"Then worry if you must, but pray for me also."

"Prayer! I pray that one day just one of mine would be answered! I shall share something with you, Willoughby, and I hope it may save you from the same fate as Joshua. Your father sought to destroy a smuggling ring; he stumbled across something far worse. I know not what, but it troubled him deeply. The last time he visited me, he warned Nathaniel 'that the rot had travelled from the deepest roots to the highest leaf of the tree'. He aimed to climb that tree and pluck out the affected leaf. Riddles … he spoke always in riddles. I have rarely seen my husband as shaken as he was by this drastic news. Joshua did climb the tree. However, he fell headlong from it. They discovered a note that he had hidden on his person. Willoughby, I shall never forgive myself if this interference results in your injury or early demise, but here is a leather wallet. It is damaged by the salt of the sea, but inside there is something you should have."

"The edge looks charred as if it has been burnt," Willoughby said as she lifted the wallet from inside the inner quilting that adorned her embroidery box.

"It was rescued from a fire." She did not explain further. "I would have you be armed with as much information as you can before you leave. I have not been at liberty to go myself, or I would have, but your uncle told me I should leave matters alone and grieve silently. He said vermin always come out of the gutters at some point." She gave it to Willoughby who turned the fragile wallet over as if he held the most precious jewel in his fingers. This was possibly the last thing his father had ever touched.

"Go where you must. Present yourself as instructed. But only read that once you are safely away from here and take the greatest of care, Willoughby."

"I will try, Aunt." He placed the wallet safely within his coat pocket.

"This is no game, Willoughby!"

He took hold of her hand. She closed her embroidery box with the other hand, as if to keep the contents safe from prying eyes. Living with Nathaniel had taught her some interesting habits.

"Sorry, Aunt, I will take care," he said sincerely.

"The powers who investigated his death put the note found inside that wallet down to the delirium of a dying man. How is that possible though? He supposedly fell to his death. Was the tide out? Did the soft sand break his fall long enough for him to write a note? If it was secreted on his person, Willoughby — when did he write it? You must look at it with fresh eyes, but not here. I am not so sure I should be telling you this." She shook her head once more. "Be on your guard, Willoughby. I fear you would be safer if you had purchased a commission in the army and were serving like your dear brother, Charles."

"Have mercy on Napoleon, Aunt. One Rossington is enough for a man, even an emperor, to cope with." Willoughby smiled and gently squeezed her hand.

"Stay. Have tea. You could sleep over and…"

"I must change and go. But I will return soon."

# Chapter 3

Beth was relieved when Wilkes moved off her. His idea of warming her had lasted but a few short horrendous minutes. Beth felt sick, as she always did.

"Get yourself back down there and finish cleaning up. It'll soon be time for you to serve in the inn, and no being overly friendly with the customers, not yet. I'll be watching you!"

Wilkes pulled on his trousers, fastened the broad leather belt that she wanted to burn, and went down the ladder back to the kitchen below.

Beth ran over to the jug of water on the old corner table. The water was cold, left there from last night. Wilkes had not used it so, although it had no warmth, it was as fresh as could be. She took the off-cut of soap from the block and the coarse cloth and cleaned herself, trying to wash him away with the feel of the harsh scrap of material against her raw skin. She hated him, hated his touch. She placed her right hand over her flat stomach and closed her eyes, stopping the tears from flowing. "Please, no! Not that. Not his!"

She shook her head, dismissing the dread of what he would do if she was with child. Beth wiped her eyes, swallowed and stood straight. She would be strong and survive. Beth pictured herself dressed fine, walking tall and away from the inn. She smiled because she loved life — if only she could live one worth having.

Willoughby nodded at the footman as he left his uncle's house, fastening his sodden greatcoat, grateful that his was made from the best quality fabric and not the cheaper pitiful version that had been sent out to some of the hapless troops fighting Napoleon in Europe. However, his thoughts about his new mission were being distracted by memories of a different kind from his last visit here. He smiled as he relived them in his mind. Perhaps he would not have to sleep in the inn tonight. He knew of a much more comfortable bed if the lady was still in town and willing. There were times when Willoughby was relieved that his uncle did not know everything about him.

Cutting through the old street of Jubbergate, Willoughby slipped down a narrow alley, stopping by the back of a half-timbered merchant's house. He knocked on the door, automatically glancing around him. After a couple of minutes the door was slowly opened by a plump looking maid who beamed at him flirtatiously when she recognised his face.

Quickly, he was invited in from the street, through the back of the medieval building. "Is your mistress in?" he asked.

"Yes, sir. She has gone early to bed." She winked cheekily at him.

"Is her good father in?" Willoughby asked.

"Oh, I'm afraid not," she smiled at him knowingly. "He has pressing business in Harrogate. Should I tell my mistress that you is waiting for her … down here?" Her wide-eyed expression was an open invitation for him to pass by her.

"No, Emily, that will not be necessary."

She flushed slightly, obviously surprised. He knew she would be flattered he had remembered a mere servant's name.

Willoughby walked along the narrow passage to the old wooden stairs. "I shall tell her myself."

Emily giggled and returned to her chores.

Willoughby climbed the stairs two at a time, his anticipation high as he approached Charlotte's bedchamber, carefully opening the door so as not to give her a fright. She lay stretched out in the softness of her bed, comfortable, surrounded by sumptuous furnishings. He entered and walked over to her; crouching by the bed, he gently stroked her hair. His body was telling him to cast off his garments and climb in next to her as he had done so easily before. He stared at the beautiful woman, the curved lines of the sheet that contoured her body, and breathed deeply at the familiar wave of pleasure that swept through him like a wave upon a shore. What was he doing here? He knew only too well: temptation, the downfall of many a good man.

"Charlotte." His voice softly spoken caused her to stir; her figure moved slowly, revealing the swell of her firm breasts. Her eyes opened, heavy lidded, a smile formed on those moist inviting lips. She held out her hand to him in welcome, asking silently for him to join her.

"Back so soon, my lover," she whispered, still half asleep.

Willoughby let his coat fall to the floor. His body longed to be with her, one last time, and then he would … no promises, no words, no more thoughts…

"Come, dear Benjamin, climb in."

"Benjamin!" Willoughby stood straight as if he had been struck in the face. *Who?* He picked up his coat and slipped it on. Who was Benjamin? He cared not. He watched her roll over, his heart suddenly heavier. How many others had felt her melt into their arms? The moment of his stupidity and weakness had passed. Her eyes already closed to the world, asleep once more, so contentedly.

His vanity had expected her to have had a tryst with him only. She had told him her lover fell in the war and could not return to marry her. He had been a fool … an easily flattered one.

"Take care, sweet Charlotte," he said softly, before turning to leave.

He quietly backed out of the room, latching the door behind him, entering the upper landing, and saw that the maid was approaching the top of the stairs. She moved silently, tiptoeing along the narrow corridor holding a lit lantern in her hand.

Willoughby stepped into the shadows, leaning into the doorway of another bedchamber, away from the servant girl's line of sight. He had no wish to have her look upon him. Yet, if Charlotte had called him by his own name and not that of another…

He was surprised when the maid stopped by Charlotte's door and pressed her ear against it, and then bending low she squinted through a key hole; fortunately the key was still within it on the inside. Seemingly disappointed that she couldn't hear or see anything, she returned downstairs to the kitchens.

He had returned, wanting to be free to choose his own path and enjoyment. He was about to go after murderers, but something in him had made him want to feel alive, before he lost himself once more in the role of Reverend Willoughby James, undercover agent and servant to the Crown. He quickly left the house passing the surprised servant without further word.

Once outside again he traversed the dirty, cramped streets eager to leave them behind and make for the fresher air of the coastal town of Whitby. Thank God his uncle did not know of his indiscretions. He would have thought Willoughby had failed before he had even begun this mission, and why? Because he had felt patronised by his uncle's words and attitude so, like a child, he had rebelled. Was he a man or a boy sulking over a hurtful truth?

Wasting no more time, he peered along the alley. Tall walls almost touched each other as the buildings' upper levels leaned out over the narrow street. The way was clear. With great care he continued swiftly. Coughing, he put his neckerchief over his mouth against the cold air.

It was his greatest wish to find the murderer of his father or those responsible, yet, he had willingly let distraction stand in his way.

Willoughby decided it would never happen again. He would find them out — or die trying to.

Willoughby wanted to catch the stagecoach to Whitby but had to cross the city first. Nearing the infamous area known as the Water Lanes, Willoughby sensed a stranger's presence before he saw him; he was being followed. He skirted a corner, then quickly stepped into an alley and waited silently for his pursuer to follow him.

Only a moment passed by before a figure entered his trap. He reached out his hand, grabbed the man by the neck and slammed him hard against the damp stone wall of the alley.

No resistance was offered. In Willoughby's other hand he held a short blade to the man's throat, pushing his face towards the daylight so he could see him clearly.

"Uncle!" Instantly, Willoughby released his grip and walked out onto the main street returning his knife to its sheath. Anger mixed with disbelief whirled within him. What the hell was his uncle playing at? He could have knifed him in self-defence. He looked around as he waited for his senses to regain some sense of order and balance.

Shadowy figures lurked ahead. Children in tattered clothes scurried here and there, mostly the unwanted result of their mothers' desperate trade, creating more mouths to feed and hence the area's poverty was expanded by the poor themselves; a perpetual trap. They scavenged for anything left by the traders as they packed up their wares.

He could have been murdered here and they would have looked the other way as his pockets were emptied, his body stripped of anything of worth.

His uncle regained his composure and stepped out of the alleyway.

"What game do you play with me?" Willoughby rounded on him.

Nathaniel brushed the dirt from his coat where it had touched against the old wall. He raised the walking stick grasped in his gloved hand. A small carriage clattered over the cobbled street towards them. Willoughby recognised the driver as the footman who had greeted him at his uncle's house.

The older man stepped forward. "Get in, Willoughby."

Obediently, but with a disgusted sigh, he did.

"To Giles Coffee House, Crombie," he ordered the driver.

In silence, they went on their way.

Once seated in a secluded corner of the establishment, Nathaniel spoke for the first time, raising an eyebrow at Willoughby. "You enjoyed your last visit to York, Willoughby? So much so, in fact, you return to make the same mistake again. Why? Are you so weak that you cannot control your own desires?" Nathaniel pulled off his gloves. "Or is that too base a question for you, 'priest'?"

Willoughby glared back as the man flung the word in his face. He knew, though, that he had no argument on which to rely.

"Perhaps you have not a sufficiently pressing business to attend to that you would prefer to play here a while longer. Should I find another man for the mission — Crombie, perhaps?" Nathaniel's expression was set like the grey stone of his new premises.

"I wished to say goodbye to a friend before leaving. That is all, sir." Willoughby stared at the impassive face opposite him.

"Is that so? Normally a handshake is all that is required," Nathaniel answered.

"Quite, I did not dally. You've made your point, sir... You followed me. You know then how short my visit was." Willoughby stared angrily. Inside, his fury was subsiding and shame was replacing the void it left. "So what do you want me to do now?" He sat upright, feeling the tall back of the settle behind his spine.

"I had intended to enter and introduce you and the woman formally, but your visit was brief. What should I expect you to do now when you are so obviously and easily distracted? I thought this was the moment you had been waiting for — to catch Joshua's murderers. Yet you choose to visit a whore! We have unfinished business, Willoughby."

Nathaniel turned and ordered their coffee.

"You still think I am fit to do your business?" Willoughby looked at his uncle, who seemed much more relaxed here than he ever had appeared to be in his own study.

"I apologise." Nathaniel's face betrayed no emotion as he spoke the unexpected words.

"For following me?" Willoughby asked.

"Not at all, Willoughby. I follow whom I choose. You did well to spring that trap, though; I carelessly walked into it in the alley. You have a firm grip and excellent reactions; mine are a little out of practice — in the field, should we say. I shall have words with Crombie, though; he was not there in my moment of need. No, I apologise for doubting your maturity. I understand you carried off your priestly persona admirably in the last mission that brought you to York, until, that is, you succumbed to Francesca's charms. She was impressed by your evasion of the truth and her inability to find out any pertinent information from you when you first met her. I believe there were other aspects of your behaviour that she was impressed with also."

Willoughby heard what the man said in silent disbelief, but found it hard to comprehend that he had unwittingly been a puppet in some sort of test.

"Francesca... Who? You are telling me that Charlotte is a known whore? Known to you?" He spoke quietly. Willoughby's disgust was rapidly turning into utter loathing. Not for her, but of himself. If he had known she was paid, or being used as his uncle's puppet he would never have ... but that was the point his uncle had so clearly made — he could not know who she worked for.

"Well, not in the sense you mean. She did not come out of the Dials of London; no, she is well-bred; very skilled in her profession thanks to having lived with a French lover. That happened after her drunkard of a husband fell into debt, so I offered her a way of keeping her in the lifestyle to which she had become accustomed. She had been struggling to find a living without the support of her lover. He lost his head over her, you could say." Nathaniel's mouth curled into a slight smile. "She was very young when she developed a taste for men. So she now works for me, enjoying it most of the time, like on your previous visit I am reliably informed. Although, your brief call this afternoon will be a disappointment to her, but a relief to me, as it shows you are not completely led by your..."

"Uncle!"

"Emotions, I was about to say."

A crooked smile settled on Nathaniel's thin lips.

"I do not wish to hear what you have been told on the matter!" Willoughby replied. "When were you informed?"

"She came to me to report your last encounter whilst you still slept like a babe. Her 'father' runs the business and we use his home as a safe house that I myself frequent often. He profits, the country has another loyal follower and Francesca plays her part well." Nathaniel's demeanour was cool, controlled, but Willoughby sensed he enjoyed playing such games with people's lives. "She is very beautiful and an attentive lover." His words were spoken with the certainty of personal knowledge.

Willoughby's anger grew. He loved his Aunt Eliza and felt sorry for her, as he remembered her conversation and the opinion she expressed about women not always being able to choose their spouses for love.

"I am not a boy and I will not be talked to in such a ..."

"Willoughby, you will listen or not listen to what I say, when I choose to say it. Is that clear? You work for me, do you not?" His uncle leaned over the table and peered into his eyes. "Think hard before you answer, because I do not want and cannot afford to have a petulant pup whelping about his mistreatment. I need a man who can take more than a little humiliation and who does not fall for the first temptress who flaunts her wares at him. You are supposed to be a man of honour, conviction and vocation. Not a rampant bull in fancy dress!"

Willoughby sighed. "I deserved that. It will not happen again."

"Good, because the fewer people who know of your true position and your true name, the safer it will be for the both of us. The ring of blackguards that your father tracked down and infiltrated all that time ago remained dormant for over five years. We were so close to breaking them. We know that is why your father was removed, so they could go to ground for a while; hence we lost the trail. A few local men and one landed gentleman were paid to take the fall for having the contraband, not the actual smuggling operation, but we could not trace the brains behind them, the power house itself and the man who provided the coin for the needed purchases to keep the thing growing. Recently, I have received information that they are back in business on an ever-growing scale, only this time they are becoming greedier; they sell not just merchandise but information, more than just the usual seafaring intelligence. They provide Napoleon with our gold!"

He paused and glanced around as his voice had risen with his heartfelt passion.

"Someone will make a mistake soon and I want to know who it is and I want you there when they do. This is why I chose you. I told you where to start. Don't ever dally when I send you out again, Willoughby! Put your brains back in your head and do not let your focus wander! You must have no direct contact with me, unless you have all the evidence I need. Then present yourself directly at my office. Do not share anything with anyone. Do you understand me?" Their eyes locked. Willoughby nodded. "Resume your persona as Reverend Willoughby James — you are to save souls in the parish of Ebton with Artemis. He will guide you as to the local knowledge. Your own life is expendable and forfeit, and will no doubt be the price you will pay should you fail or become careless. Officially you are no more than a priest and no one has any proof otherwise, unless you behave recklessly."

"And when I succeed?" Willoughby asked.

"Then, dear Willoughby, you will have your aunt's and my undying gratitude and an annual sum of five thousand pounds settled upon you for life from the family estates, and on your next birthday do not forget that the great lodge at Rossington Hall becomes legally yours, along with your inheritance from your father's estate. On that you have my word. But you do not have to work for me unless your duty to your country wills it. These things will be yours anyway."

"I choose to work for you, Uncle. But tell me, once Napoleon is defeated, do I have the right to live my own life as I choose to?"

"I do not force you, do I?"

"No, but that was not what I asked, sir." Willoughby stared back at Nathaniel's expressionless face.

"Once you are in receipt of all that your father and uncle have willed you, you shall be free to choose to take your final vows, whether to be ordained as a priest and make your aunt proud or to walk away from the church you so abhor."

"I have never said I abhor the church or God. I merely seek the right to choose my own way in life and live it as I wish to."

"Of course you will and must, dear boy, of course! You are a free man, not a slave, are you not?" Nathaniel's manner relaxed. "Very well said and very noble; perhaps you should speak in the open fields to the common man as do the rebels."

"Then let us pray for my success," Willoughby said sincerely.

"Good man, start behaving as a noble man of the cloth and less as a rutting buffoon! Now drink your coffee and you can return to the coaching inn." Nathaniel stood up, hardly waiting for Willoughby to finish.

As he said his farewells outside the coffee house, shaking hands in a proper and polite manner, Willoughby watched his uncle leave, with one phrase running through his mind. He repeated the words slowly over to himself, "Never trust anyone." He watched his uncle's back, watched the straight figure he had grown up in the presence of and wondered what he was really like. Did anyone other than Eliza really know him? "Trust!" He said the word over to himself quietly. Trust our Lord, possibly, but he doubted if he would ever trust a mortal soul again.

# Chapter 4

Willoughby had had a long journey and a tiring day and so returned to the Phoenix Inn. He needed a good night's rest and then to make his arrangements quickly for leaving the city early the next day. Willoughby opened the narrow low door and entered the smoky gloom of the tavern. The air was thick with the smell of burning cheap tallow candles, stale sweat of the unwashed travellers and locals alike, mixed with the heady aroma of ale and the smoke from many a pipe.

"Drink, mister?" The lively voice of a young woman drew his attention to the slight figure who had appeared at his side. Willoughby acknowledged her politely as he saw her long lashes flutter slightly as she greeted him.

"Can I get you anything … anything at all … mister?" Her impish grin was well practiced, if not genuine. Her actions and words seemed mature enough for any harridan, but as he looked down he saw there was something about her eyes that betrayed her true feelings. Willoughby sensed she was merely acting out a part that had been taught to her by someone more experienced. Or was he just feeling jaded after his unexpected meeting with his uncle? Still fresh-faced, there was something desperate about the young woman that was certainly not at ease with her surroundings.

"You could tell me if you have a room free and when the stagecoach to Whitby leaves, miss."

"Well I can, but it won't do you much good, mister, as today's have all gone."

Willoughby looked at the small figure standing before him; she was petite, which only served to make her look more vulnerable within the surroundings of the inn.

"When then?" he asked.

"You could try the mail coach; that goes tonight. Leaves at dark and you'd be there by morning, and it's always on time." She glanced over her shoulder and, seeing that nobody was listening, leaned towards him. "Mind, it goes over the moors, where owls hoot and 'things' roam in the night. If I were you I'd stick to the daylight hours, best be safe, eh? The guard on the post even has a blunderbuss, but some say that there are things shot that it goes straight through!" As if suddenly realising she had spoken out of turn, she took a small step backwards, for a moment looking a little lost whilst waiting for his reaction.

Willoughby grinned at her concern regarding the journey over the moors, even if her head was filled with superstitious nonsense. He ran his fingers through his hair and sighed. He wanted to be out of the place but was tired.

"Sorry, mister. That's just the way it is. Perhaps you'd take some stew and a tankard of best ale to cheer you up?" She looked up at him, large brown eyes staring at his from a pale pixie-like face. "You could stay the night here. I'd get the room ready for you." She looked at him hopefully.

He placed a hand on her shoulder. "You have nothing to apologise for. It is, as you say, the way it is. I believe the guards are merely protecting the mail they carry from would-be thieves ... not strange 'things', but dangerous people."

"Lass! When you've finished flirting with the customers, I'd like serving, you hear me!" A stocky brute of a man sitting at a table in the corner of the inn, surrounded by a group of his drinking friends, was shouting across to the young wench.

Willoughby saw him staring jealously over. She ran over to them instantly with a pitcher of ale in her hands.

"Sorry, I was just being polite, Mr Wilkes." Her apology was met with derision, and a firm slap on her buttocks.

She poured out the man's drink, before being pulled roughly onto his lap.

Willoughby could sense her fear despite her best attempts to adopt a relaxed manner. She used her hands on the man's arm, struggling to pull herself free, but he held her tightly.

"Show me you're sorry then, Beth, for neglecting your master." He nodded at his friend who immediately pinned her arms back behind her whilst the man kissed her roughly, grabbing at her thinly clad breasts, delighting in her hapless squeals.

Willoughby walked over to the table and addressed the man directly.

"Release her!"

The girl's tear-stained face looked up at him as her provocateur kept his hands firmly clenched on her body.

"Me and Beth are good friends, aren't we, lass?" He turned her face to Willoughby. "Tell the nosey stranger how close we is. How I've taught you everything you know." He laughed in her face, his friends joining in the chorus.

She did not speak, but stared through wide, fearful eyes at Willoughby, her pleas for his help like silent prayers, intangible, yet their strength unmistakable.

"Still shy are we? Well everyone has to learn their trade and she's no exception! She's mine! My name is Wilkes... Mr Irwin Wilkes, remember it as you leave, sir... Whilst you still can." Wilkes continued to laugh, enjoying the power he had over his victim.

Willoughby noted that not the entire group joined in with his cruel taunts. He could also see the shame on Beth's face.

"Let her go," he said calmly, his words hiding the rising anger within.

"Be on your way, mister, or we'll send you on it."

Willoughby leaned forward, his hands near the edge of the table. His greatcoat fell open, his priestly uniform visible.

The men around the table looked amongst each other and two shifted very uneasily. "Bloody hell, whatever next!"

"Leave her, Irwin, you can toy with her anytime," one man said, then made his apologies to Willoughby and left forthwith. The others sniggered at the man's sudden display of conscience.

Wilkes released Beth and nodded to his friend who let loose her arms. "We don't need a priest. I wasn't proposing to her." He laughed heartily and so did his friends, whilst Beth ran off like a frightened rabbit to find a hole in which to hide.

"You find ganging up on a defenceless woman entertaining, do you?" Willoughby stared at the man.

"Yes — what man wouldn't? Anyways, she ain't defenceless. She's a woman grown and serves up more than drinks here. She's my whore, man! So if you want to give out any sermons I suggest you do it to her. We 'sinners' succumb to the temptation of a woman's body, so I begs your forgiveness … and bids you good day as we have no reason to detain you further." Wilkes feigned a pathetically humble expression and a half bow, but his eyes were fixed on Willoughby.

"It's not *my* forgiveness you need to seek." Willoughby wanted to upturn the table and grab the wretch by his neck but was only too aware how odd that would appear for a man of the cloth. He had a mission to attend to. This was yet another time-wasting distraction, but not one from which he could have walked idly away. He hoped he had not just failed another of his uncle's tests. So much for a night's rest in a warm room. Francesca had her path dictated by Nathaniel; this wench, Beth, by the likes of Wilkes. The similarities were glaring to Willoughby, as much as the supposed comfort one seemingly had over the other's harsh existence. Their fate was to be the same.

"She is a young woman, treat her so!" Willoughby stood straight and slowly turned to leave the inn. Mr Irwin Wilkes was a name he would not forget. Willoughby hated bullies, having seen too much of them during his schooling. One day, he promised, he would see that Wilkes would answer for his cruelty.

Willoughby found another inn nearby, booked a room and slept soundly after what had been a very long and troublesome day.


Beth ran to the back of the inn. She kept busy and out of Wilkes's sight. He would be drunk soon enough, and then she could help roll him up to bed. But her heart lifted because of her stranger. The man who had come off the coach, her gentleman, had stood ground for her. She had never had a champion before.

Once Wilkes was safe and sound, snoring in his bed, she would find out where the man had gone. Something about him drew her to him. Their paths were meant to cross. With gathering excitement and that rare feeling of 'hope' she set to waiting for Wilkes to call for his bed.

Every minute that passed by she was more eager to find her gentleman again.

Willoughby left the inn early the next morning, pondering the purchase of a horse or maybe renting a post-chaise.

"Mister?" The voice interrupted his thoughts. Beth's nervous appearance from the alley nearby made Willoughby wish he had finished what he had started and taught the man a lesson from the previous night. Why she should seek him out, he did not know, but she still looked scared.

"Beth, wasn't it? Can I help you?"

She shrugged, as if not sure what to say, and stepped forwards, closing the gap between them.

"Is he always so cruel?" Willoughby already knew the answer. There were thousands of wenches trapped like her — they had to perform and please their keepers or be beaten, or worse.

"He'll be right mad now, when he wakes and remembers, but thank you for trying to help me. You was quite a hero." She smiled as Willoughby shook his head and grinned at the idea. "I was thinking if you go to Jenson's, next to Braithwaite's the coppersmiths, you could rent out his post-chaise or hire a horse from there." She sniffed and discreetly wiped a tear away from her eye.

The more Willoughby looked at her, the more desperate she seemed to become.

"Step into the light here, Beth."

Nervously she edged forwards.

"How old are you?" he asked.

"Not sure." She looked down at her tattered skirt. "No one ever kept count, but I'm old enough, I guess."

"For what?" Willoughby looked at her and wished he could help her out of this hole she had to exist in.

She looked sideways then her impish eyes found his and she shrugged. "I'm no child, sir," she added wistfully.

"Who is this Wilkes and what is he to you?"

"He owns the tavern, mister." She looked up at him, hopeful, and Willoughby realised his time-consuming distraction was not about to be cast off lightly by her silent plea for help or his own conscience's desire to answer it. Willoughby believed strongly that sometimes people are placed in your path for a reason.

Beth's reply made Willoughby realise he now had another problem to deal with. Frustration rose within him because, as often happened, he had a conflict within him. He cared for the downtrodden, yet his missions meant he had to often walk past.

"How did you come to be here?"

"I was given work here from the orphanage, mister. I grew up there when my ma perished."

"Would you like to leave the inn for good?"

"I can't. I've nowhere to go." Coyly she looked up at him, eyes watery and her bottom lip trembling. She was wretched enough already in Willoughby's eyes, without making more effort to touch his heart.

Willoughby felt in his pocket, turning over a coin in his fingers. Her wise eyes looked at him knowingly.

"Don't, mister... He'll find it and I'll get a beating if I don't hand it over to him, or a ... if I do. Either way, I'd lose. You best hang on to it." Seemingly resolved to her fate, Beth slumped her shoulders and started to walk slowly back up the alley towards The Phoenix Inn.

"Do they have any legal hold on you — signed papers, anything?" Willoughby asked.

"No, they bought me from old Gilbert, keeper of the place, by the back door, so to speak. He made his money selling off bastards and orphans that were declared dead, or never registered proper on arrival. Wilkes will be mad as hell if I did a runner but there's no papers concerning me. I'd just never do it on me own because if I'd be found I'd ... well, I'd be better off dead." She turned her back to him, stooped even lower and slowly moved off.

"Show me where this Jenson's is then." He knew she was desperate for him to offer a way out.

Her agile body turned instantly and her head shot up. "May as well get hanged for a sheep as a lamb then, I suppose!" she announced, and started walking back along the alley, head held high, as she stepped out into the main street trying to look confident.

Willoughby followed her, wondering what on earth he was going to do with a young woman. Her manner seemed to have been instantly transformed, her steps were light and she smiled warmly and genuinely at him... 'Daughter of Eve', he mused, trying to cast an image of Nathaniel's angry countenance from his mind.

# Chapter 5

Beth walked slightly ahead of Willoughby. After a few moment's brisk walking, she showed Willoughby a coaching house next to Braithwaite's. Pointing to a well-dressed gentleman in his middle years who was talking to one of the stablehands, she turned to face Willoughby. "Ask that man there, he's Mr Jenson. He's not bad, but he likes to make a good profit." A look of sadness returned to her eyes.

"Thank you."

"I hope your God protects you." Beth fidgeted with her raggedy boots, anxiously rubbing the toe of one against the scuffed surface of the other.

"He's yours too, you know. I don't have exclusivity to him, believe me." He ignored her doubtful expression. "Is there nowhere you know of where you could go to and be safe?" Willoughby asked her.

"If I did have somewhere to go, don't you think I'd be there? I don't like being ... touched by him, you know," she snapped, before adding awkwardly, "They'd find me and take me back, for sure. I may as well go willing, or it'll be the worse for me. Beatings can be long or short, hard or brutal, so I'll go get mine before it's too bad." She stared up at him. "Thanks for your kindness. You're a gentleman for sure. I never had no one look out for me before. I hope you meet a real lady one day who'll look out for you too." She swallowed and took a step forward after giving him one last long look.

Willoughby smiled wryly to himself at her guile. He did not like Wilkes and hated the idea the man would have his way. He needed time to think, but that was the one thing he lacked.

"Wait here, let me sort out my transport, Beth, then I'll help you." Willoughby saw her eyes shine again.

"You don't need to do that, mister." Her words betrayed her gratitude to him. She desperately wanted him to help her; that was obvious. "I'm tough, you know."

He gazed back at her, but knew she was wrong; they had not crushed her spirit yet. It appeared she was Wilkes's play thing, for now. Her future was destined to become that of a whore, soon enough. She could still be saved. "I know, and it would be much easier for me if I didn't, but Beth, I give you my word that I will. You are not going back to that inn. I'll speak with the Mother at the convent. Perhaps she could offer you her protection. Stay here, I shall return in minutes." Willoughby patted her reassuringly and started to cross the muddy road.

"Like hell you will!" Beth muttered. "I ain't going in there!" She was both angry and disappointed. Why had she got her hopes up, risked a beating for a bloody priest who would drop her in with his 'sisters'. Did he have no idea of how they would view 'her sins'? And she would have to stay here, in York. Here she had no chance of escaping Wilkes.

Whilst Willoughby approached the man who had been pointed out as Mr Jenson, Beth disappeared into the narrow streets. He glanced back over his shoulder and realised that she had vanished.

"Damnation!" he swore to himself. He had wanted to help her, not scare her off. Why hadn't he kept his intentions to himself? He should have known better. But surely a disciplined life in a convent would be better than a wasted one at the hands and whim of Wilkes?

"Good morning, sir. How can I help you on this fine day?" the cheerful owner asked as he saw Willoughby approach.

Willoughby looked at the vehicle being cleaned in the cobbled yard. It was in good order. He saw the postilion in the stables wearing his bright red-buttoned jacket, and smiled to himself; he had found his transport. "I wish to rent the post-chaise to take me to Whitby as soon as possible."

"Then good fortune is indeed shining upon you, sir." He took a closer look at Willoughby and grinned sheepishly. "Or perhaps God has guided your path, because, due to a cancellation, I have one post-chaise available, if you do not mind sharing with one other passenger."

"No, I do not mind. Should we discuss the cost?" Willoughby reached inside his pocket. The man stepped into his narrow office built on the end of a stable block. He opened a ledger and showed him the tariff, which was calculated per mile, depending on the number of horses that were used to pull the vehicle.

Willoughby shook the man's hand, the detail agreed and coin paid. Jenson left him and Willoughby placed his bag safely on the vehicle with the aid of the postilion. He wandered a few paces back to the street, watching and waiting, his mind turned instantly to the wallet that had been his father's. He wanted a quiet moment, a private place where he could open it, consider it reverently like a precious artefact, one that linked to his heart. Not here, not now, but very soon the contents of it would be revealed. A last message, perhaps, from his father to him. Could he really be the one to bring justice for the murder? He would do his best and in the process, to please Nathaniel and his father's memory, he would also do his duty.

Willoughby's attention was suddenly caught by a flurry of activity as the people at the other side of the street stirred. His interest switched to a different place, and someone else's problem.

"Come 'ere, yer little rat!"

Willoughby heard the coarse voice of Wilkes shouting from across the road and turned to see that the man was giving chase. Willoughby knew who his prey would be even though she was not visible. Willoughby stepped backwards by the side of the post-chaise, but he could not turn away; he had got the wench into trouble and he would hold to his promise to help her.

He took to his heels and followed the commotion. His thoughts could wait; now was the time for action.

# Chapter 6

Beth caught a glimpse of Wilkes in the distance and panicked. She ran down a narrow snicket. She thought that she was in for a thorough thrashing when she returned to the inn, but he had come out into the street and that meant he was in a blinding rage. Beth had turned and run, but her steps faltered, slipping on the grimy cobblestones, as she crossed the roads. He had her. There was no through way. She was completely trapped.

"Where you going to run to now, my sweet? You've lost what sense you had if you think you can outsmart Irwin Wilkes." With deliberate movements, he rolled back his shirt sleeves, relishing her fear as she cowered in the corner.

Beth's breathing quickened; she knew the mistake had been hers. Why had she placed any faith in the damned priest? He was handsome, but why would that turn her senses; she hated men and none more than the one who stood before her now. Damn men and damn her day-dreaming of her knight who would come to the inn on a coach and take her off to be a lady.

Beth couldn't stop her body from shaking. She was more scared than she had ever been in her life. There was no excuse in Wilkes's book for running away, she knew that, and yet still she had gone on a whim. Wilkes had told her often enough what he'd do. She wanted to scream for help, but knew this time no one would come — no one would ever come for the likes of her. Once she had tried to escape ... only the once, and then she had promised never to again. Then she had been given bruises, but this time she'd carry the marks from her mistake through the rest of her life, and all because of an interfering priest whose idea of help was to offer her up as a sacrifice to nuns. Perhaps, as she stared at Wilkes, she should have taken him up on his offer.

"Mr Wilkes, I wasn't running... Honest, I wasn't running, Mr Wilkes… I was coming back to you … honest! That priest man wanted to know where to get a horse, that's all. I thought he'd pay me … us, honest!"

"Honest — you? There's no good lying, Beth. You can say sorry to me and the lads later, lass — that's to come. It's time you earned your keep proper like the other whores. Why, you've bitten the hand what feeds you twice over, Beth, and no one gets away with that — them's the rules. This time you'll not forget. You've lost your favoured spot. You won't be Wilkes's girl anymore. You can earn your coin in the inn and then you'll realise how lucky you was."

Wilkes stepped forward.

Beth could not form words, her mouth opened, but nothing came out.

"I told you, you don't ever cross me. There's a lot of nasty folk out here who would take advantage of a young wench out on her own." He gripped his belt's buckle, flicking the leather like a snake in the air; it made a loud cracking sound near her. It had the desired effect as Beth curled into an anxious ball, her slim body jumping involuntarily at the noise.

She made one final plea, forcing the words out. "I only went to show the priest where to go, to get him out of town. I was coming straight back, Mr Wilkes, honest. You saw me coming, didn't you? He was a preacher man, Mr Wilkes. They always poke their noses in other folks' business, sir. He didn't know no better." Beth spoke imploringly, daring to look up, but her eyes were watching the leather as he flicked it again in the air; the sharp noise became louder and sharper as he stepped closer to her. Beth cringed at the memory of its feel. It took months for the mark to go last time.

"You wouldn't know what honest was. Your sort never do."

Staggering, Beth forced herself to stand up, her legs quivering. She held both arms out in front of her, palms upwards, pleading with all her might, trying to get the man to see reason, her reason, but she was fighting a losing battle because he had a vicious temper and had a taste for beatings. She swallowed hard, and nervously glanced to one side of him and then the other, wondering if there was the faintest hope that she could slip past him and escape into the town again; the convent was starting to appeal.

"You won't ever consider trying to do a runner again, girl. You ain't got nowhere to go. You belong to me and the inn and it's time you remembered it. After this, Beth, if you even think of taking to your heels, I'll hobble you, and then even old Abel would be able to catch you up."

She was a fool. Too late to do anything now, she thought, but then … she saw him, like an apparition in black, and with him hope returned. The stranger, her interfering priest, blocked out the daylight at the entrance to the narrow alley. His tall figure was easily recognisable. Her mood changed in a flash. She stood up straight, folding her arms, seeing Wilkes's expression change to one of confusion as he watched her.

"You're a bloody guardian angel, that's what you is, mister," Beth shouted past Wilkes.

"Don't think you can trick me so easily, Beth. I know all your sneaky ways, and I ain't falling for that one." Wilkes raised the strap high above his shoulder height, ready to strike. Willoughby was fast. He grabbed Wilkes's wrist below the hand that held the belt, wrenching it behind the man's back, clenching his other fist into a hard ball. Wilkes turned, but

Willoughby landed a firm punch on the man's jaw. He dropped to the muddy earth like a rag doll, his legs folding beneath him. It was one quick effective blow. It would not take the man long to figure out who had brought him down.

Beth ran to Willoughby, her arms outstretched, and hugged him tightly. Then she stepped back, kicking out at Wilkes's prone body lying in the dirt.

"There was no need for that," Willoughby gently rebuked her as he led Beth away.

"Believe me, Reverend, there was!" Beth snapped back and forced her hand into Willoughby's. "Anyhow, it was you who floored him; you did real good, mister."

"Perhaps, Beth. I have to leave here... I suppose that now means we both have to leave here."

Beth smiled. "It might be best, unless you want a murder on your conscience. He'll be beyond mad this time and he'll come for both of us. He has eyes everywhere. A coin here, a threat there, and they'll soon have you pegged. I won't be no bother to you, honest," Beth added brightly.

Willoughby glanced down at her. "Why do I doubt that?"

"Have faith," she whispered and winked impishly back at him.

"And you have some respect," he answered. The smile dropped from her lips, but her eyes still shone brightly with that same glint of hope he had seen creep into them when they had talked in the alleyway by the side of the inn.

They retraced their steps to Jenson's where there was no sign of the post-chaise — the yard was empty. Willoughby ran his hand through his hair again.

"You'll go bald if you keeps doing that."

"Beth, you are causing me more problems than you know." Willoughby remembered his uncle's warning about the fairer sex. Somehow he doubted even his uncle would have credited he could have been taken in by this one. He would have to find a home for her, and quickly. Then, he could finally be about his own business.

"What now?" Beth asked.

"Now, I should consider taking you to the convent." Willoughby stared at her, but he had a firm grip on her hand this time. The mention of the convent had her pulling away, trying to release his grip. He ignored her efforts, but added, "We had better leave before Mr Wilkes rounds up his friends, Beth. Where is the nearest establishment like Mr Jenson's? Don't worry; I don't think the nuns deserve you."

"You'll not find one, but we could try the gate. Hitch a ride on a cart or something," Beth offered optimistically.

"Firstly, I have to retrieve my bag. Then we shall see." If he left her at the convent it would be the first place Wilkes might search — or try to. Willoughby would have no way of knowing if he could get at her. Besides, he had no wish to spread Wilkes's menace to innocents.

He walked over to Mr Jenson who looked very surprised to see him. "My good man, what are you still doing here?"

"Something came up; I take it that the coach left on time?" Willoughby asked politely.

"Yes, indeed it did, but I cannot refund your fare as..." Mr Jenson coloured slightly.

"That is not necessary, sir. It was my mistake. I took too long finishing my business. However, I do need my belongings." Willoughby saw Jenson's face flush an even deeper red.

"Your bag was still placed on the post-chaise, sir. I presumed you would be travelling too. When it left, I had no idea you were not already inside the vehicle or I would have asked them to wait for you." The man fidgeted nervously with his watch chain.

Willoughby shook his head. "It went on the vehicle, without me?"

"Well … yes…"

Accepting this was also his mistake, Willoughby nodded. "I should have realised it would leave on time." He looked at Beth who had a suitably soulful expression on her face. "Do you have a horse I could rent? I shall catch up with it and then your postilion can return with the animal when his journey is completed. Would that be agreeable to you?"

"Perfectly, sir." Jenson went straight to the stables and had a sound animal saddled and made ready. Honourably, he refused to accept anything other than a nominal fee for its hire.

Willoughby swung himself into the saddle. Beth grabbed the reins, a look of panic on her face. "You can't leave me here! Please don't take me to the convent. He'll find me for sure. Wilkes'll kill me for this, honest to God! Women like me can just disappear without trace, you must know that."

Willoughby leaned forwards and held out his arm to her. She grabbed at it anxiously and he pulled her up in front of him. Enclosed within his open coat, she sat holding tightly on to the horse's mane. Willoughby had lost enough time and he was expecting a less than gracious Mr Irwin Wilkes to emerge from the alley at any moment, so with no more than a polite nod to Jensen, he rode off. They went through the old stone-walled gates, he gave the animal a firm kick and let it have its head. Beth squealed with joy at the new experience.

Once outside the city walls and on the open road, Willoughby laughed at her, for here he soon began to see a change from the frightened rabbit he had met to a bird that had just been shown how to fly; freedom soaked into her slight body. Her pale pallor was being replaced with a rosier glow. His uncle would say his compassion was his weakness; if so, it was one he valued.

Willoughby would have to unearth the truth of the past, whilst accepting the complications of the present. He followed the road leaving the city to gain distance at the gallop, but then branched off a mile or so outside.

"Why have you left the road when you can see the post-chaise straight ahead?" Beth twisted around in the saddle as best she could to look up at Willoughby.

"Patience, little one, and you will see why." Willoughby rode the horse into a copse of trees on a hillock away from the main roadway that offered excellent views over the vale. From there he looked back to the city built of wood and stone ensconced within its crumbling medieval walls. A few moments went by and Beth fidgeted anxiously, impatient to be on their way. Willoughby fixed his eyes ahead as he aimed to get away as quickly as he could. Life was always chaotic — he grinned — but it was better than being bored.

Beth was a strong character, of that he was certain; he would not abandon her to the fury of Wilkes. Willoughby's hunch was justified when he saw a group of three riders leaving the city, following the post-chaise at great speed.

"Wilkes! If he's chasing us this far then he surely has murder on his mind! What do we do?" Beth clung to Willoughby's arm as it encircled her waist, holding her securely.

"We wait, we watch, and when the time is right, we continue on our way." He dismounted and helped Beth down. He tied the horse's reins to the branch of a tree so that it was well out of sight.

Once this was done, he lay down; Beth followed his example and the two of them lay upon the grass, their eyes firmly focussed on the riders gradually catching up with the post-chaise on the main road south.

They stayed silent for a few moments until Beth broke the peace. "Why are you a priest?" Beth asked, as she played with some long grass, picking and plaiting it.

"Because…" He glanced at her. "That is a strange question. Would you ask a surgeon or doctor why he was one? Or even a soldier for that matter?"

"Nah, what I mean is that you don't act like one, though, do you?" Beth persisted, as she continued to twiddle with the grass.

"I frequently act like one. I don't usually end up hiding in the trees with a…"

"An innkeeper's whore!" she jumped in. Her eyes were downcast as she scrunched up the piece of grass in her hand.

"I was going to say with a vulnerable young woman, whilst being pursued by a group of ruffians." He kept his eyes firmly on his pursuers.

"More's the pity then." Beth's voice was filled with conviction.

"Why?" Willoughby asked.

"You're too good at it to be wasted in a pulpit."

"Priests don't stay in a pulpit all their lives. They have duties and the Word of God to spread. I somehow think your experience of the priesthood, like that of life outside that tavern, is somewhat limited."

There was a silence while Beth looked thoughtfully at the blade of grass. "Oh, I've met a priest before…"

He glanced at her quickly, noting that her face had hardened again, like the tone of her voice, and her mouth was screwed up in an almost childlike countenance.

"Do you think He'll forgive me then? God I mean … not Wilkes or the priest," she asked.

"For what?" Willoughby asked. He looked back to the road.

"For doing stuff… You know. Wilkes, he made me go to his bed. Said if I didn't that I could entertain his customers." She shrugged her shoulders dismissively, whilst continuing to stare at another twisted blade of grass wrapped around her fingers. "We is supposed to stay where we've been put in life, aren't we? Accepting our lot, eh?" She looked at him, as if she wanted his blessing to be free of it. It was another silent plea for a different type of freedom, though he had helped her already.

"I think we are all able to learn and change, Beth. Jesus spoke to all kinds of people, didn't he? And it is not 'We is', but 'We are'."

She looked blankly at him and shrugged her shoulders.

"Are you sorry that you did those things?" Willoughby asked.

"Yes, most of them, except for kicking Wilkes in the alley." She grinned at him. "I didn't choose me life, you know. It was do it, or face worse or starve. That ain't much of a choice."

"Then, I think, if you ask Him in your prayers, you'll find He already has," he said, and added, "Ask Him to understand about Wilkes, I'm sure He will. It should be that 'isn't' much of a choice, not 'ain't'."

"When I say me prayers!" Beth repeated, and then flopped back on the grass, giggling to herself.

Willoughby ignored her as his attention was fully taken up by what was happening on the road as the riders caught up with the post-chaise.

The riders approached the vehicle, stopped it, looked inside and then seemed to question the postilion who engaged in some banter with them. Having been unsuccessful in their quest, they started back. Willoughby waited patiently until Wilkes was well on his way to the city before making a move to remount. He was grateful that they had not realised his bag was still on it.

"He'll get drunk now and be really horrible to everyone for days."

"I don't think anyone will notice the difference. He seems to be a permanently angry man." Willoughby reached down to Beth and pulled her up onto the horse so she was once again sitting upon it in front of him.

"What are we going to tell Jacob?" Beth asked, holding on to the horse's mane for dear life.

"Jacob?" Willoughby asked, staring at her as she stroked the animal's neck.

"Yeh, that's him, the driver of the chaise. What will we tell him? I best stay out of sight. He comes to the inn most nights, when he can, barring Sundays of course."

"This Jacob knows you and Wilkes then?" Willoughby did not move the horse as he thought through his options. He had not realised there would be any connection between the two.

"Yeh, I'll say. Him and Wilkes, well, they're in business, should we call it."

Willoughby looked down at his new friend, seeing her for the first time as less of a burden. She had local knowledge and if the 'business' they were involved with was the trade, then perhaps Beth would earn her keep in a very different way. She could provide him with local knowledge. That in itself was quite some revelation. "Explain your meaning, Beth, or walk back to the city now." Willoughby's voice was deliberately serious.

"You wouldn't!" Beth snapped.

"Yes, I would!" He stared at her, all humour and good nature hidden.

Beth paused, clearly thinking hard, then came to a decision. "Swear you won't tell a soul I told on 'em." Beth skewed herself around so as to see his face clearly.

"I swear I will send you back if you do not confide your meaning to me now. I think there will be no need to say how I know if it comes to passing the information on."

"On the Bible itself?" she persisted.

"Beth!" Willoughby snapped at her.

"It's important, mister."

"Yes it is. So say or go!"

Beth swallowed. "He drives for Wilkes and takes messages back and fore to the coast," Beth explained, and then added, "Remember your promise not to say I said owt."

"I always do. Not to say anything, Beth, not owt. What kind of messages?"

"Messages about deliveries and such — you know, landings of things: kegs, tea, silks. He helps pass on the word so that the tub men are met and the goods can be spread amongst his buyers." She stared at the distant city. "No one is ever supposed to tell on them. They do horrible things to those who they think have turned traitor. I'm trusting you, priest."

"Mister James will do. Mr Willoughby James." Willoughby knew the carriers of the goods that were brought ashore along the flat sandy north east beaches were met by a network of vehicles and stashed along the old routes; he had travelled the area trying to pick out some of them, when he could. Yet never had he managed to come so close to Ebton. The country, criss-crossed as it was by the old paths, known locally as the 'monks' trods', were perfect for hiding contraband. The moors were treacherous to cross; you had to know the pathways that generations of farmers, monks and traders had used.

"Then we go straight to Whitby. I'll get you out of sight and meet the chaise in the old town, where it will stop near the inn. He can take this horse back and I'll collect my bag. I won't be in Whitby long before I move on again," Willoughby said thoughtfully, then walked the horse out of the cover.

"What about me?" Beth asked.

"Good question, Beth. What about you?" Willoughby kicked the horse to a gallop and offered no answer. He would have to deal with his first problem, to reclaim his things, and then he would decide what to do about Beth. He would make contacts as his uncle had stipulated, as the mock priest, then would hang up his uniform. He was a marked man. From then on he would be just Mr Willoughby James — a gentleman in his own right.

"You ain't going to ditch me with some mad nuns, or at a tavern, 'cos I tell you if you do I'll run!" Beth was almost shouting as they travelled.

"Where would you run to?" Willoughby asked calmly.

"Don't know. Don't care, but I ain't going to be locked away again." Beth sniffed and Willoughby realised that this time her distress was genuine.

He placed a firm hand around her waist. He would buy her the best meal she had ever eaten once they arrived safely at the coast.

He leaned his head toward hers so that his words would be heard above the movement of the animal they rode, and not blown away by the wind. "You're not going to be locked away, Beth. But I need you to obey me, respect me, and in turn I shall respect you."

Beth sniffed and her tears were seemingly gone. "I ain't never thought I'd have a priest respect me. Things is lookin' up, eh?"

# Chapter 7

Willoughby made his way toward Whitby and the rugged north-eastern coast, crossing the vale and climbing the steep hills up to the open moor. Here the countryside changed dramatically. At first Beth's head seemed to dart from side to side as she took it all in, but then fatigue dampened her curiosity and she nestled into his body's warmth again.

"Can we have a rest somewhere? My legs ache. We've ridden all morning." Beth had been wriggling for the past half an hour and Willoughby was tired of her perpetual fidgeting.

"I was just thinking the same thing. We'll stop at the inn on the moor road and have something to eat. We are well ahead of the post-chaise, but one thing, Beth — you must come when I say without question, stay where I tell you to and do nothing to bring attention to yourself."

"What else would I do and where else am I going to go?" Beth asked.

"Just stay quiet, and out of trouble. See if you can manage that."

Willoughby rode into the yard of the next inn they came across, leaving the horse in the stable behind, and quietly entered the low building, ducking below the lintel across the rear doorway. Willoughby walked in first with Beth's slight figure slipping into the shadows of the room behind him. It was a low cruck-built building, a well-used stopping point by travellers along this lonely road.

He gestured to Beth to sit on a high backed settle in the gloomiest corner of the room. Willoughby approached the serving counter, ordering a plate of cheese, ham and bread and a jug of ale. He noticed a man wearing a tricorn hat, casually smoking his clay pipe and gazing out of the low window staring northwards, his back to the serving hatch where Willoughby was standing.

Willoughby paid the innkeeper for the food, watching the stranger as the innkeeper took his coin, but neither man spoke or acknowledged him.

"Friendly, the locals," Willoughby commented quietly, as he sat down next to Beth again, his larger frame shielding her from view. She wasted no time before eagerly biting into the food.

"You wouldn't want to make conversation with him, Mister James. He's trouble — big trouble." Beth's voice was no more than a whisper. She nodded at the man in the tricorn hat.

"Why is that? Who is he, Beth?" Willoughby asked her, still keeping his voice low.

"That's Oberon Spratt. Don't mention his name to no one." Beth gulped down some ale. "He terrifies people, just by his very presence. I hope he didn't see me." Her voice was hardly audible.

Willoughby glanced to where the man Spratt was sitting, his legs outstretched, resting his feet on the table in front of him. The long boots he wore Willoughby suspected had once belonged to an officer. The rest of his clothes were old, dirty and unfashionable. Yet, his manner oozed confidence.

"He doesn't look very terrifying to me," Willoughby muttered, then bit into his bread with enthusiasm after watching Beth attack hers, but was soon disappointed as the taste and texture lacked freshness. Still it was food and, after seeing the way Beth savoured every bite, he renewed his promise to feed her a decent meal once they were safely in Whitby.

"He makes Wilkes look like an angel, believe me, so don't go messing with him." She glanced beyond him. "Folks like him have an extra sense; they sees and hears everything." Beth shrank back into the seat.

"Whatever he is, he is only human, Beth, no more, no less, with all the limitations that brings."

He watched Spratt and tried to follow his viewpoint to determine what was so fascinating that held the man's attention, but he could not see through the small window panels.

A few minutes later, a large carriage pulled up outside the inn. The footman entered and approached the innkeeper.

Willoughby watched Spratt as he walked towards the doorway. He stopped momentarily and stared at Willoughby. Beth was hiding behind him, using Willoughby's body and the shadows like a shield.

"Good day, sir." Willoughby smiled pleasantly at him.

The man's fine features lifted slightly into a smile, acknowledging him. Then he continued walking without a word and left the inn. The footman, seemingly happy with the response from the innkeeper, shook the man's hand and bid him farewell.

The coach had something written on the door — an 'RI'. It pulled away.

"That's real grand that is. One day I'd like to travel in a carriage like that." Beth looked up at Willoughby impishly. "Instead of sharing the back of an old nag."

"Your choice, Beth. You could have stayed in York." Willoughby was watching outside the doorway. "Come on, we best be getting on our way."

"I need the privy. You go get the horse and I'll meet you outside." Beth jumped up and made her way through the back of the inn.

Willoughby paused on the threshold to admire the view across the moors. It changed quickly as did the harsh weather up here, but it held a certain rugged beauty. He stepped one pace beyond the threshold before turning to go and retrieve the horse.

"Travelling far, sir?" The voice surprised him. The man Spratt was leaning against the stone wall, one foot placed flat against it, still chewing on his pipe.

Willoughby looked at him, noting he had the most unusual and striking grey eyes.

"Only to the coast, not much further now... And you?" Willoughby placed his hat on his head. He was being equally casual in his manner.

"Have we met before, sir?" The stranger was looking quite closely at Willoughby's face.

"I don't think so, sir."

Spratt stared impassively at him. "Best be getting on your way before the weather closes in. This isn't the place to be caught out in a storm."

"No, I should think not." Willoughby's attention turned to the road as he saw riders approaching. There appeared to be three, riding at speed toward them. "They're in a hurry," Willoughby commented.

"Talking to yourself now," Beth's voice surprised him.

"No." Willoughby looked around for the elusive figure of Mr Spratt. He had disappeared like the proverbial 'will o' the wisp'. "Well, I wasn't. Did you see Spratt?"

"You think I'd stand here, bold as brass, if I had known Oberon Spratt was here?" She looked around anxiously but

Willoughby's attention was on the approaching riders. He realised they were dragoons.

"Go get the horse, Beth, and stay around the side of the inn until I come for you."

In an instant Beth was gone.

The three men dismounted. Willoughby was greeted with a pistol pointed at his torso.

"What is the meaning of this?" he demanded.

"Mr Oberon Spratt, I arrest you for crimes of..."

"Then you arrest the wrong man. I am a reverend, Mr Willoughby James; you have made a grave mistake, I fear." Willoughby looked up at the young lieutenant whose face was already flushed from the exertion of the ride.

"Reverend ... James?" he asked Willoughby, without lowering his pistol.

"Yes." Willoughby stared at the young man.

"Can you prove this?" He waved the pistol at Willoughby who was still standing with his hands raised to the side.

"Not without moving, no. However, if you will lower your weapon, then I can."

"The innkeeper says he was here earlier, but has left." One of the soldiers came back out of the inn. The man looked at his lieutenant and then at Willoughby. "Is this one of his men, sir?"

"I suspect so. We shall take him with us to Whitby. We can interrogate him there."

"If you would escort me to the offices of Major Husk of the dragoons in Whitby I would indeed be beholden to you, sir, as he is the gentleman I am travelling to see," Willoughby answered calmly and saw the surprise in the young lieutenant's eyes.

"What business do you have with him?" he asked.

"I really think that is a matter for the major and I," Willoughby replied.

"Search him," the lieutenant ordered, visibly angry at Willoughby's refusal to share the information with him.

The soldier searched Willoughby's greatcoat pockets. He found nothing but his purse, a folded scrap of paper, and a small pistol. The man held it up. His uniform was now clear for the lieutenant to see. The man appeared to colour slightly, in surprise.

"A priest with a pistol, sir?" The lieutenant watched him closely.

"These are dangerous roads, sir, and we all must protect ourselves." Willoughby stared blankly back at the men as he spoke, successfully controlling his anger.

The weapon was lowered. "We shall escort you to Whitby to see the major, and, if your story is true, I shall apologise for the misunderstanding. However, if he has no knowledge of you, you shall be a guest in our gaol, and you shall answer any question I see fit to ask. Now fetch your horse and make no attempt to escape or I shall have you shot down."

Willoughby walked over to the stables where his horse was still tethered. Beth was hiding deep inside the ramshackle building. He saw her peering over an old wagon at him. "Stay here," he mouthed at her, then mounted the animal and re-joined the three soldiers. He was not given his pistol back but was made to ride between the lieutenant and his sergeant whilst the other soldier followed on behind.

# Chapter 8

Willoughby had not been taken far when the sound of gunshot erupted ahead of them; flashes appeared to the left and right of the road as if the moor had ignited.

"The men are being attacked, sir!" the sergeant shouted and tightened his hold on his horse's reins in readiness for kicking him onwards, clearly anxious to go to their aid. Willoughby could tell by his assured manner that he was an old soldier used to reacting to the skirmishes of war, unlike the inexperienced officer he was forced, by his rank, to obey.

The lieutenant was hesitating, but the sergeant was not; he obviously wanted to be after them. "Should we ride to their aid — *now* — sir?" he asked.

"Yes, yes, of course, but I should stay with the prisoner," he added, and looked severely across at Willoughby.

"The 'prisoner', sir, is not the man we were sent here to arrest. He is a priest. If you pardon my asking, sir, but do you think the captain will look kindly upon his detention … sir?" The sergeant seemed barely able to restrain himself as he looked accusingly at the young officer.

"Look, my man," the lieutenant turned away from the sergeant and addressed Willoughby, "take this as a warning of how serious we are about cracking down on the trade in these parts. *If* you are truly an innocent man, unknowing of the brigand's activities within this region, then I ask that you use your position to spread that word to those of your flock who are not so. I shall give you the benefit of the doubt, this time, as my duty calls me elsewhere." He handed Willoughby's pistol back to him with a firm hand. "Let me give you some sound advice: you should think twice before using that."

"I am not in the habit of shooting people, lieutenant. It is merely a deterrent," Willoughby explained.

The lieutenant faced the direction the gunshots came from and shouted boldly, "Men, follow me!" He rode off at speed as silence fell, the volley over.

The sergeant shook his head and exchanged a look of despair with Willoughby. "God help me!" he said and followed his superior along with the other soldier.

Willoughby, wasting no more time, doubled back to the inn; he made the horse gallop as fast as the animal could until the building was in sight. Only then did his pace slow. He walked his horse around the back to the stable where he had left Beth. The afternoon was gloomy and posed the ever present threat of rain.

Looking around the small yard and then the stable, Willoughby could not see Beth anywhere. He stood perfectly still and listened quietly. He thought he heard a sound from behind some bales of hay. Stepping between two of them Willoughby saw a glimmer of light catch something, a slight movement in the far corner. He heard the unmistakable sound of heavily stifled sobs. Moving one more bale a broader beam fell onto the shivering figure of Beth. She was hugging her knees to her chest, appearing small — a quivering, scared young woman. Willoughby's heart filled with silent rage at what life had done to her.

"Beth," he spoke softly to her. She had not heard him approach over the sound of her own sobs.

Her head lifted up.

"Jesu... Reverend, you came back!" Her eyes opened wide and she wiped her face with the back of her hands. In the next moment she stood up and launched herself at him, clinging to his body as if she had not believed he was real.

"I told you that I'd come back. Now, I think it would be an excellent idea if we both left here without further delay. It's getting a sight too busy for my liking." He patted her head gently and felt a tenderness towards her that surprised him. He could not abandon her. Willoughby realised he had given Beth a rare gift — that of hope.

They must follow the old moor tracks down to the coast road and avoid the skirmish at all costs. This held risk, but he thought he could remember the routes which he had seen mapped out by another agent the previous summer. Willoughby had studied the terrain of the area in case he was sent there. The roads were rough, but locals had traversed the area for centuries on foot and horse.

"Listen, Beth. We have to travel to the coast by a dangerous path. You must stay alert as there seems to be more travellers out today than I had hoped for." He lifted her onto the horse.

"The ghosts of old monks walk them. I know … I've heard the travellers at the inn, scared out of their minds by what they've seen up here." Beth's face was recovering its normal colour and animation.

"Well, then, we shall take care not to disturb them … don't want any more company, do we? I think I already have enough!" Willoughby winked at her, walking the horse along the road a few yards until he saw an old flagstone to the right that was almost overgrown by moss. This was, he knew, the beginning of one of the trods. If he had to, he would follow it on foot, leading Beth upon the horse.

They travelled in silence. Willoughby noticed that Beth was calm once more, seemingly loving being atop the animal.

"Something's blocking the path up ahead," Beth whispered.

"Yes, I see it." Willoughby dismounted, taking to his feet as he had planned to, and saw marks where something had been dragged. His eyes scanned the ground. Then he bent his knee and felt the ground itself. They were not recent, perhaps already a day old. It was then he saw the lifeless hand, cold and stiff. The rest of the man's body lay where he had fallen behind a gorse bush. He wore the habit of an old monk. So much for people seeing ghosts, Willoughby thought. He must have been one of the smugglers' ring, a tub man, left there from the previous night's activities but, as yet, he lay undiscovered. A bullet wound was visible in his back. He looked at the man's face. It was not someone he recognised. He must have been running away from the path after dropping his keg. Willoughby returned to the horse without saying a word about the body to Beth, who sat nervously looking around her. These were harsh times when a man would risk his life or another's easily for the payment of a contraband run. Land workers were low paid, crops were not reliable and fishermen depended on a decent catch. To fill in the gaps in their earnings lugging or stashing contraband was a very lucrative alternative.

"It was a discarded barrel of brandy. We better be swift, Beth, as someone will return for it, I have no doubt about that." He distorted the truth.

"We could strap it to the nag, Mr James, sir?" She looked eagerly at him. "It'd fetch a price and I'd not let on."

"No!" He kept walking.

"Shame," she said, but did not press her ideas further.

They made steady progress until light faded. Beth was shivering with fear, Willoughby realised, and not because of the cold. He made for the crumbling walls of a long deserted castle keep. The once grand structure now appeared to be no more than an empty shell, but its broken walls would provide them with shelter. Their bodies would have to provide what warmth they could share.

"We sleep here," he announced and dismounted.

"Here!" Beth's eyes widened as she slipped off the horse, steadied by his arm and shrank back to Willoughby's side, as she peered into the ivy clad shadows of the walls. "God help us, for if the shadows of the ancients walk these walls, we'll not wake up the morrow!"

"Have faith, little one, at least in me if nothing else." Willoughby secured the horse's reins to an old protruding iron hook as Beth watched him. Her back straightened. He was handsome, he was strong and he was looking out for her — what more faith did she need? She watched him remove his greatcoat, and gesture for her to go to him.

"We nestle together here and sleep for a few hours. You need not fear me, Beth."

She lay down next to him and was soon enveloped by his arms and coat. She said nothing, snuggled up close and wished that the night could last a lot longer than a few hours as safety and warmth were hers at last.

In the distance, an abbey's ancient ruins stood boldly on the horizon, clear for all to see for miles around. The air had the distinctive taste of the sea to it.

"I've never seen the sea before!" Beth exclaimed.

"It is both beautiful and treacherous. You will come to Whitby, but you must learn a few new rules." Willoughby felt very tired, but it was refreshing to see they had found their destination.

She twisted her head to see his face clearly. "I ain't livin' with nuns!" she declared adamantly.

"No, you're not." He grinned at her. "However, you must blend into the background whilst I return the horse and retrieve my baggage."

"I'm good at that."

"We have to find you some respectable warm attire." Willoughby looked at her tattered frock.

"You mean, you don't find me beautiful, mister?" She fluttered her eyelashes at him.

He stared back. She looked down shame-faced, as if she had sensed his thoughts, then blankly stared straight ahead.

"That wasn't funny. I'm sorry, Mr James. I'll never do that to you again, ever." She looked the other way.

"Not just to me, Beth. I hope you will never have to show your favours to anyone until the day you are happily wed."

"Wed, me? Fine chance I have of that!" Beth replied.

"One day, you will find someone who will love you for yourself."

Willoughby kicked the horse onwards.

# Chapter 9

Riding down the steep bank into Whitby, Willoughby breathed deeply, invigorated as the wind blew in over the German Ocean. Beth seemed exhilarated by either the place or her new found freedom. Nobody appeared to pay them any attention, as all about them was a mass of activity, noise, colour, with a myriad of contrasting smells.

Willoughby eased Beth down off the horse as they arrived outside a hotel. He noted with some surprise the coach that had stopped at the inn on the moor moving off from the front of the building and wondered who it belonged to. He temporarily dismissed the thought — this was a very busy port. It was, after all, the regular route for travellers. Willoughby committed the design, the ornate letters 'RI', to his memory, as surely it would be well known in what was a small but important shipbuilding and whaling port.

"Stay here, Beth. Speak to no one and I'll see if the chaise is still in the yard." The girl nodded but shivered as she stood bracing herself against the stiff sea breeze. He removed his greatcoat and placed it around her shoulders. It swamped her thin frame. Willoughby walked the horse behind the large brick building, its hooves clattering loudly on the cobbled stones. There were a few fine carriages stabled behind; it was obviously a place frequented by the local gentry. He saw the Jenson post-chaise and was relieved. He wanted to return the animal as he had no wish to be accused of being a horse thief as well as whatever charge Wilkes may be trying to conjure up in his maddened mind. That was not the covert start to a clandestine mission his uncle had demanded.

"Can I help you, mister?" the stablehand asked him.

"Yes, I have a horse to return to the driver of that chaise," Willoughby explained, and nodded towards the vehicle.

"If you leave the horse here, I'll make sure that Jacob takes the animal back to York with him when he returns." The man took the reins. "He'll be in the Old Launch Inn if you want to see him. I'll see to it that it's fed and watered."

Willoughby gave the man a coin. "Tell me, do you know if a bag was left on the chaise when it arrived?" he asked.

"Yes, it was taken into the inn, sir." He pointed to the door.

Willoughby wondered if the people inside were being careful with his belongings or rifling through them. Willoughby looked back at the man. "The grand coach that just left here, a moment since, who does it belong to?"

"The one just now?" the man asked, seemingly surprised by the question.

"Yes, that one."

"Why, that is the Ingham's carriage. I thought that most folk around here knew that," the man said, as he unsaddled the horse.

"Perhaps they do," Willoughby said calmly and smiled, "but I am not from around these parts."

The man nodded apologetically. "No, Reverend ... course not. He owns mills and the alum works and a good stretch of land thereabouts."

He collected his bag and felt relieved that at least Jenson's man was honest enough to have left it there for collection.

Willoughby returned to Beth. "It's time you had a damn good hot meal! Come," he said. She happily did, seemingly content to follow where ever Willoughby led.

# Chapter 10

Willoughby crossed the old bridge that joined the east and west side of the harbour as it crossed the river Esk. He followed the road around to a market square.

"Quickly, Beth, look amongst these for some decent garments that will fit you," Willoughby said, but saw her hesitate and so he asked the stall holder for her. Each one he inspected as to quality and reasonable cleanliness, and then he haggled for them, knowing the trader was glad of his business. Willoughby had more idea of what was fashionably acceptable and would make her look respectable than Beth had. Once she had a bundle of decent second-hand garments under her arm and a new pair of boots, they entered a low roofed building to the side of a small yard off one of the busy lanes. Steam rose from the chimney balanced at an odd angle in its uneven roof.

"Good evening, could you tell me if it would be convenient for the young lady to use the bath-house to freshen up?" Willoughby asked the woman just inside the building, ignoring the gasp he heard escape Beth's lips.

The woman looked her up and down and nodded.

Taking back his greatcoat from Beth, Willoughby said, "Good," and paid the coin. She then pointed to the door at the back of the building. Beth, with a tight-lipped reluctant stare directed at Willoughby, followed the large woman who had appeared through the open doorway.

Beth looked back at Willoughby; he saw anger replaced by fear in her eyes.

"I will be here."

Beth nodded and succumbed to her fate, gripping her bundle tightly.

Willoughby passed the woman an extra coin. "Make sure you get through that hair, comb any lice out of it and have it brushed fine. I want her cleaned up and made seemly. She will need to stay at a respectable hotel and must not look like she serves within it."

The woman took the coin gratefully, smiled widely and rolled up her sleeves. "You leave it to Nell. I'll have her looking like a duchess for you in no time. See you in an hour, eh." She shushed him out into the yard and closed the door. Willoughby grinned, realising that poor Beth was in for quite a shock, but also knowing that it was needed. He ignored the distant sound of swearing as Nell set to her task and went to find some food to appease his new charge with when she was released from what would be her idea of purgatory, no doubt. He walked the streets until he had familiarised himself with the location of the barracks and the whereabouts of his contact. Willoughby still wore his greatcoat. His identity would need to be that of Reverend James to see the major, but he had no wish to meet the lieutenant again beforehand, so he kept his coat on and melted into the crowd.

An hour passed by as he scouted the area. He watched vessels being unloaded to see if any still sat low in the water; a secret cargo hidden, perhaps, to be landed at night.

Willoughby turned to make his way back and could have sworn he caught sight of a man in a tricorn hat making his way up Baxtergate toward the old Launch Inn.

Beth stepped out to meet him as he returned to the yard with her old clothes tucked under her arm in a small bundle, with clean brushed up hair under her newly acquired hat. It was starting to wisp slightly as it dried; the slight colour of flame matched the look in her eyes as she stared at him. The dirty brown colour had been replaced with a rich auburn hue with fiery highlights.

"You came back then — to see what skin I got left!"

Willoughby pulled the bundle from under her arm. He tossed it to Nell. "Burn them!"

Nell grinned.

Beth went to storm out of the narrow yard into the street but Willoughby took a hold of her arm. For one minute she glared at him, her eyes meeting his in total defiance.

"Breathe deeply... Do it."

She opened her mouth to answer him back, but he raised his eyebrows in a gentle warning and she then did as he asked. After four deep breaths her temper seemed to have stilled.

"Now, calm yourself. Walk with me as a respectable lady would; one who can walk at my side, who can put her shoulders back, hold her back straight and look up to meet the world.

The anger in her stilled as she took in one more deep breath; accepting his words, she straightened her posture and, amazingly to Willoughby, changed her appearance in an instant.

He took Beth along the narrow streets on the east side of the harbour. Here they cut down a narrow snicket, passing another coaching inn, following the main street almost to the harbour. Cupping her elbow, Willoughby steered Beth up a bank as the road swerved to the right, leading to steep steps that took them up past the church of St Mary's perched high on the headland, overlooking the harbour below.

At the top of the rise they stopped a few moments. Looking out to sea in the evening sunshine Willoughby stared at the busy harbour below. He wondered how many sailors on the whaling, fishing and merchant ships had looked upon the stark ruins of the abbey as a heart-warming sight on their return journey home.

Months spent working all hours on a merciless sea ended when the fishermen returned home, seeing these two prominent landmarks. The abbey and the church must have been such a joy to their hearts. Willoughby smiled as he realised Beth had placed her hand in his. "Majestic, isn't it?" he commented as he studied the activity below.

"Bloody cold or damned windy would be better descriptions," Beth answered as she braced herself against the strong gusts that swept in from the sea, tucking in close to his side. "So now you've seen the view, can we go back down to somewhere warm where there's a fire before I catch me death?" She clung keenly to her newly purchased second-hand bonnet.

Willoughby looked at her. No doubt after her ordeal she was feeling the cold more than he thought. "I wanted to talk to you somewhere out of earshot. Let's find a sheltered spot." He walked her to the overgrown façade of the once great abbey. Standing in the long shadow of the tower, Beth looked ill at ease.

"Doesn't this place give you the jitters?" Beth said, as she tiptoed over parts of the broken masonry to stand with him against the stone wall.

"Absolutely not, the opposite is true. It was a place of devout worship for centuries." He sat down on the remains of a column. "It fills me with a sense of wonder and peace."

"You is a strange one, Mr Willoughby. There's been bad blood spilt here over the years and bad blood don't rest easy when they've been wronged!" Beth leaned against a tall colonnade and crossed her arms in front of her. "It fills me with more than a bad sense of trouble. I bet it's been used for a lot of unholy stuff since it fell apart." She looked around her uneasily. "Look at that big house. Do you reckon they'll set their dogs on us for trespass? I don't think this air is good. There's too much of it, it's not natural."

"You've spent too much time locked away in an orphanage and that inn. You've forgotten what your lungs are for."

"I can feel it. I sense these things ... bad things. I was only with him for a few months, you know. I'm still young and I mean he ain't done ... so many times and..." She looked away. She shrugged. "Long enough, I guess. So what is it you want to say?" Beth returned to her impish smile; she had switched mood again like the wind when it changes direction. She blew hot or cold but never lukewarm, and he knew that his words were not going to come easily to him or be received keenly by her.

"Listen, Beth, I made enquiries at the hotel and he informed me that there is a large country house near here that is opening up after being closed for the past few months. The family are taking on staff now. I want you to try to find work there." He stood before her, hoping she would see that this was an excellent opportunity for her to improve her place in life, but also strongly aware that he had shown her a glimpse of freedom. She had taken to it well and servitude would offer her little to calm that spirit of hers.

"So, you want to rid yourself of me?" She stood up straight, facing him squarely and leaned forward, poking his chest with her finger as she spoke to him. "Why did you bother bringing me all the way here, scrubbing me raw, if it was just to cast me off again? What's wrong, Mr James, won't your congregation like you having a 'sinner' like me in tow?" Her words were filled with bitterness.

"No, that is not what I meant..." Willoughby began to try to explain as much as he could. "I am between two different worlds at present. I need to think a lot of things through before I decide if I wish to be ordained a priest. In the meantime, I need to fulfil a promise to a friend and visit some people in this area." Willoughby paused as he saw a flicker of interest in Beth's eyes. "I want you to find work in the house for a few weeks, and then I shall return. You can decide then if you wish to stay there, or leave with me. But, Beth, you will have to settle down somewhere."

"Really?" Beth said, obviously unsure of his words.

"Really!" he promised, praying he would not break his word and make her trust in people disappear for good. For Heaven knew she'd had little enough reason to believe in anyone else in her life.

"Then I suppose I could try." Beth sat down again and tapped her toes together.

"Good, now tell me what you know of the trade around here?" Willoughby thought he had slipped his question in innocently enough, but Beth's eyes met his, and she grinned back at him.

"What interest would that be to you?" She folded her arms in front of her.

"I've saved you from a life worse than a dog's; you owe me at least a little bit of respect and..."

"Oh, I respect you, but I also think that you are going to get into a whole lot of trouble asking folk questions like that," Beth said flatly.

"I'm not asking 'folk', Beth, I'm asking you. Tell me what you know of Wilkes and his connections here and I'll be better able to look after myself. Who is the man Spratt, or what is he?" Willoughby saw a fearful look cross Beth's face.

"I don't know much about him." She looked around them nervously as if they were being spied upon. "No one does. That's how he keeps it; that's how it works."

"Then tell me what it is you do know about him," Willoughby persisted.

"You is one nosy priest ... or near priest, Mr James, sir. Spratt is not the leader; he works for a man, one who has money and knows rich folk. No one but Spratt knows who he is. He oversees the loads from Whitby to Ebton and beyond. He knows the pannier tracks like the scars on his own hand. Jacob is just one of many links between the city and the coast. I hears they meet at the Old Launch Inn, here in Whitby — contacts, traders and the like — and messages go back and fore the whole time. Wilkes is just one of his distributors amongst the inns and houses in the area. Anyone who speaks out, or asks too many questions, ends up dead." She looked at him with what could only be interpreted as open concern. "Don't try to preach to them types, or you'll meet your God real quick. They don't like strangers nosing around here. They ain't got consciences. Don't even try to get into their inn; you'll not come out the side door in the same state you entered the front one if you do. They don't want folks knowing their business. They'd take you out the side alley to a boat and then ... well, let's just say I hope you like fish!"

"Beth, how do you know about the side door if you've not been here before?"

"I listen to Wilkes, and I've heard him talk to Spratt in the cellar."

Willoughby looked at Beth. She had led a very precarious existence. Her life would be forfeit if they ever found her again — of this he had no doubt.

"I want you to be in a safe place in the large house I told you about. I'll find lodgings and I'll let you know if I move on. Can you read?" He placed a hand on her shoulder. He was anxious to see Husk and begin his next quest.

Beth laughed an empty laugh. "Sure, I was schooled in me letters right after I was shown how to…"

"Yes, I can see that was a stupid question," Willoughby admitted. "In which case, I must find a way of leaving a message for you."

# Chapter 11

Willoughby escorted Beth carefully back to the church of St Mary, this time entering through its stone doorway. He walked her inside and seated her on one of the boxed-in pews. Beth almost recoiled as he opened the small door to the enclosed seat. They had been made so that each pew was private in the main church; the gallery above looked down upon the regimented rows. She perched in the corner as if a thunderbolt would strike her down for merely daring to enter God's house. Willoughby could see the panic in her eyes.

"Beth, you have nothing to fear here. Stay hidden in the corner. I will leave you for a short while. Make that scrubbing down you had a symbol of a new beginning. Let it wash Wilkes and your past away."

"Is it really so simple?"

"If you will it to be so, then it can become so."

"No, please … don't go…" Her eyes fixed upon him. In her new clothes, she looked so different; Willoughby was taken by the warm flecks in her hair. It, like her, had so many colours to add to the world. She was a young woman who should be setting out on a future of her own, finding a man who could value her, not someone who carried so many scars from her recent past.

He glanced at his bag. "I will leave this here with you. My father's spy-glass, my most precious possession, is within it. Here, look at it…" He showed her that he was not lying in the hope that his trust in her would be loyally returned. "I will return for both of you, but I have someone I must see."

She nodded. He closed the pew box securely and quickly left.

Beth was far from comfortable with her surroundings. She edged her way to the end of the pew. Staring at Willoughby's bag, she had been touched by his willingness to trust her. Her finger played with one of her loose hairs. It felt so good. Admittedly, she had rebelled at being attacked by the old witch, Nell, but she felt clean. Is this what real ladies felt like, she wondered. The clothes, though not new, were warm and better made than any she had worn before. Their seams were not threadbare. Looking at Willoughby's bag, she wondered if she should hide it and run away, but she liked the idea of being entrusted with its keeping. It was something personal of his and he had given it into her care. She dared to look around her, taking in the majestic nature of the building and awkwardly ask 'Him', whoever 'He' was, if it would be possible for her to stay in Willoughby's house. She could be his housekeeper, she added, but her heart told her she would love to be so much more. Willoughby was a gentleman and she was a fallen woman, but he treated her as if he respected her. Beth almost laughed aloud at the notion, but then remembered where she was. She settled for asking to be his housekeeper. So she could always be near him.

He was a mystery to her; a priest who walked in the shadows. Beth took hold of Willoughby's bag and let herself out; if anyone should ask her what she was doing she would say returning the bag to its owner.

Feeling lost and alone, Beth wandered aimlessly along the narrow ways of the town, hauling his bag with her. So long as she had something of his with her, then there was a chance that he might not leave her behind again. Beth would go back to the church after she had walked a ways and got some fresh air. It was strange. People were not staring at her. A man even doffed his high hat as he entered a shop. She glanced to her side as if expecting to see some respectable folk standing by her. Is that what a scrub up and some warm clothes does for you? She smiled, her back straightening without her realising it, her head lifting a little higher, allowing herself to meet people's eyes more often.

She watched the ships lined up across the entrance to the natural harbour. On the river along the harbour side, men were loading and unloading goods ready for the next tide to take the vessels back out to sea. She looked up towards the abbey, remembering the conversation between herself and Willoughby. Life wasn't fair. She could be good for him, for she would never look at another. Beth shrugged, her posture stooped again; he would never look at her with anything other than pity mixed with shame. He was a good honest man. What to do now? With the light now going, she stared back at the church on the hill. Why not just do as he bid her? At least whilst she did, he would stay with her.

Beth gamely made her way back up the steps, secretly hoping she might find Willoughby already waiting in there. She stood before the imposing church which was perched proudly on the cliff. "I think I should act as a lady, no shame. Start afresh, he said," she muttered the words to herself, smiling as she held on tightly to her hat with one hand and Willoughby's bag with the other. Once inside the arch she followed the aisle to the right and walked along the narrow aisle with the boxed in pews to the left and right. Some had name plaques on them. Beth wished she could read them. She imagined having her own name and carriage like the grand one with the lettering on the door. Her name ... Beth...? No... Elizabeth... James... Mrs Elizabeth James, she smiled. She loved to dream, but this one was impossible, definitely beyond her reach. Beth held the bag close to her body instead.

She glanced around her, and then entered the anonymous steep sided wooden pew that Willoughby had left her in and there she sat guarding his belongings in the church below the ruins of the old abbey.

Beth stared about her. This was a strange church. When she had attended services in the Hall with the other orphans, the seating was open, on the floor. The poor sat at the back, those who owned the place were seated on benches in the front. She had thought they were on the proper pews. Here small groups of people were seated in their own little box pews unable to see other worshippers, but they could all look up to the pulpit. She tucked the bag under the seat and then, unable to settle, decided to explore the gallery. Walking quietly up the wooden staircase to the right of the entrance to the church, she admired the view down into the maze-like assortment of pews. As she stared at pulpit and seating alike, she could clearly see where Willoughby's bag had been hidden and felt strangely at peace.

Footsteps sounded on the slab stones as someone else entered the building. Beth shrank back into the shadows.

Willoughby approached the gated archway of the barracks yard. He was stopped by a soldier.

"I need to see Major Husk," Willoughby explained.

"Does he expect you?" The soldier eyed him with interest.

Willoughby smiled, letting his uniform act, as it so often did, as a pass into another world of acceptance.

"Yes."

"Who wants him?"

"The son of a family friend."

The man ordered a corporal to escort Willoughby across the square to a stone two storey building at its rear. He was led up a flight of spiral stone stairs to a first floor tower room. The soldier knocked firmly on the old oak door and waited for a response.

"Enter!"

The corporal announced Willoughby's presence and Willoughby entered.

He stood to the left inside the room to allow another soldier to leave, carrying an empty bottle. Willoughby could smell the brandy as he passed. With his slight build, the man easily squeezed between them, nervously looking down at his feet, avoiding Willoughby's gaze as he ran at the double down the flight of stairs.

Willoughby unintentionally followed the man's gaze and was surprised at the state of his boots. In the ranks at war, men wore what they could to survive, but here he would have expected better discipline.

"Come in, my dear young man." The warmth in the words surprised Willoughby as the bearded officer gestured for him to sit down opposite his desk. The major's chair nestled into the curve of a window in the tower; from there he had an excellent view of everything that entered the square fort below. He could at any moment turn around and watch the activity below clearly.

"I come on behalf of Lord Rossington, I am Mr Willoughby James..."

"Welcome. Care for a drink?" The major poured the warm liquid out into the cup that had been brought in on a silver tray, then opened a crystal decanter of brandy and poured some into his cup of tea. "Just a little nip protects one against the cold, you know. Damn chilly place this is. When that blasted wind comes across the German Ocean it finds every crack in this place to blow through. Would you care to partake?" He offered Willoughby some, but he declined.

"How is Lord Rossington keeping?" the major inquired.

"He is well and sends you his good wishes, Major."

The major sat back in his chair and considered Willoughby for a while. "You look every inch your father's son."

"Thank you," Willoughby answered. "I had little enough time to know him, but I take that as a compliment."

"As so you should." Major Husk carefully removed a folded piece of paper from inside his tobacco pouch. "I have written to Nathaniel for long enough asking for these blackguards to be investigated. I never let your father's work go completely cold. Now, these are some of God's children who have done really well for themselves within the region at the time of his death and since. Some are the charitable type, some have donated to the lesser, one even brought up a bastard child as his own niece, and some care for nought but themselves and could do with a man of God to set them straight." He leaned over the desk and whispered to Willoughby, "I believe that they have one thing in common, but I can't find it, nor prove it. Take your time to memorise these few names, they are all I have left to show for five years of work. Joshua and I both stumbled across them at the same time. I was a young soldier eager and ambitious for promotion and full of ideology, but your father was a good man interested only in the truth. Take care of this list — I hand the quest to you."

"Where had he been prior to his 'accident'?" Willoughby asked.

"He'd taken to walking along the cliff path, not where he was found, but south of Ebton, watching the alum works. However, he had other reasons for his journey there." The major chuckled and gulped down his drink in one swig. "He was taken with a beautiful woman... " The major's right hand suddenly grabbed at his throat, the other to his chest. He breathed in deeply, and then reached out for Willoughby's sleeve from across the desk; his eyes stared wildly at him. "Sim..." Husk's portly frame slumped to the floor, grabbing repeatedly at his own neck and chest, gasping for air, his pallor turning grey, and his skin clammy. Willoughby bent forward and shouted out for help, but stone walls and the thick wooden door stopped his cry being heard.

Willoughby opened it wide and shouted down the stairs. But by the time he returned, the major was already beyond saving, choking his last breath. Willoughby placed the small piece of paper into his boot and waited the long silent seconds it took for the soldier who had shown him in to return.

"What happened here?" the corporal demanded to know, flushed with panic as he saw the man lying motionless on the floor.

"He was talking to me one minute and then had some sort of fit. He just ... died! His heart gave out! Who gave him that drink — the soldier with the scruffy boots? Think man! Could it be poisoned? Where is the man who brought that drink in here?"

Willoughby moved toward the door. The soldier pointed a pistol at him. "Stay here," he ordered. Willoughby responded with an affirmative nod, and the soldier left to raise the alarm.

Willoughby waited for him to leave, then sniffed the tea and brandy. Poison. He knew the scent. The man had been 'removed', like his father, but by whom? Why now? He searched the man's pockets for any other clue that could lead him to one of the names on the list, but there was nothing else to help to him. Either way, Willoughby had much to do.

He ran down the stairs and stepped through an open doorway into an empty office, closing the door behind him until he heard the feet of running soldiers pass by. They were led up the stairs by a nervous young lieutenant. "Detain that priest whilst we have the major examined by the surgeon. He must have slipped the poison into the major's drink."

Willoughby waited, then eased the door open a crack. When he was out of the line of vision of the last two soldiers he made his way down and skirted the courtyard. He stayed calm, looking for a way to slip out of a barracks full of soldiers on alert. A wagon was circling the yard, turning, making ready to leave. Willoughby fell into step with it; he calmly escaped by walking at the side of the leaving wagon as evening turned to night and light faded and slipped out through the large gates. Once outside the stark walls, he crossed the street and cut through the crowds, making his way to the narrow alleyways that criss-crossed the town.

He needed his clothes and so made directly for the abbey stairs. He hoped it would be possible to retrieve his bag swiftly without endangering Beth further. He raced up the stairs as quickly as he could. He may not have wanted company on his mission; however, he could now see how the presence of another person might definitely make the perfect cover for him, as the soldiers would be searching the streets for a solitary priest.

Beth saw a soldier rush in to join the first man waiting below.

"Well," he panted. "Man, it's done, and I want me money now. I did the job just as you asked." The voice was breathless and anxious.

Beth listened, hardly daring to breathe lest she be heard. She leaned slightly forward peering over the gallery to the pews below. All she could see was the corner of a hat — a tricorn. Spratt! Surely not, she reasoned. Her hands felt clammy and started to shake. Whatever would he be doing in a church?

"Listen, you cowardly whelp, when I hears it's done, then I'll give you your dues. Now what about the list. The man said he had one?" There was an uneasy pause. "Did you find the list of names? I told you that was what you had to get off him." Spratt's voice was gaining a nasty tone, his anger barely under control. It was a tone she had heard before.

"There was no list." The other man's voice was hesitant.

"Well did you search him, thorough like?" Spratt persisted, but the reply was vague and uncertain.

She heard the soldier being slammed through a wooden door and onto a pew. Quickly she leaned back, as she did not want them to know that Beth from the Phoenix Inn was there.

"I was going to, but then he had a visitor and I had to go before he drank the stuff…"

"Could you not have stayed and acted like a true servant, made your damn self invisible?"

"As soon as the priest entered, they told me to push off like." The man's voice had risen higher as fear gripped him.

She heard a 'thwack' followed by a sharp noise and a voice cried out in pain.

"Ahhh! I … did … me best," he snivelled. Beth suspected he had broken the man's nose. "If they'd found me out I'd be for the rope, or worse, Van Diemen's Land!"

"It's just as well that we're in a house of God, or I'd despatch you to him in a blink of an eye. Find out if they both took the brandy. That would solve two problems in one go. Wait a minute — this priest, what did he look like?"

"He was dressed in black, and…" *Thwack.*

"They all bloody well wear black, you fool!"

"He wasn't local, he were younger like." The man sniffed again.

"Tell me, did he have fair hair?"

"Yes, I think so…"

"Damnation, I could have done the job better myself."

The men stood up and she heard their footsteps leaving the church, their voices trailed off out of earshot. It was Willoughby they had spoken of, it had to be. But did this mean he too was dead? Beth's heart was racing. What if he was? What should she do? The bag; Beth must hide it, and herself. She ran back down the stairs and returned to the pew. Carefully she removed the bag from its hiding place. She looked at the altar. "God! Forgive me what I have done, you know I wasn't willing… I need your help!"

A hand touched her shoulder and she nearly screamed as she formed a fist at her side ready to punch anyone in a tricorn hat who may have returned unnoticed.

Willoughby took Beth's small hand in his. "It's all right, Beth, it's only me."

"Willoughby … you're safe!" She stepped over the bag and realised she was all but ready to hug him out of a sense of pure relief, when she noticed how flushed his face was after the climb to the church at the top of the steep steps.

"I need you to bear with me a moment whilst I change in there … the vestry."

He looked surprised when Beth agreed, immediately lifting the bag and pushing it at him. "Good idea, quickly."

He wasted no time, disappearing into the back of the church, taking his belongings with him.

Beth tried to calm herself. Her life was moving at such a pace that she was struggling to keep up with events. She had put herself in the protection of a man who now appeared to be hiding from murderers. She paced around the church impatiently whilst she waited for Willoughby to return to her and explain. One of them, Spratt, knew her too well.

She heard more footsteps approaching. A mature priest entered the church and smiled at her politely. "I am sorry, my dear. Were you waiting here to see me?" His face was weather worn but he seemed kindly in manner.

"No, I mean, I was admiring your church, whilst I rested ... and waited." Beth spoke clearly, hoping her voice would travel around the empty church.

"It is indeed a beautiful place, and has withstood many a treacherous storm, unlike some of the poor souls in our graveyard, alas."

Beth nodded and looked down, praying that Willoughby would return soon. Her wish was granted as he boldly entered from the main entrance where the priest himself had come in only moments before.

Both of them turned to see a well-dressed young man in dark trousers and a stylishly tailored jacket that could be seen under his overcoat, flapping open as he strode in. His hair was pulled back and tied at the neck. It appeared darker but Beth realised he had combed oil through it to gain the effect; it was mainly hidden under a fashionable hat which, together with the elegant cane and cravat, made him look every inch a true gentlemen. Beth stared at him in open admiration.

"I do apologise for taking so long, my dear little sister, but the view from the abbey is positively breath-taking." He turned to the priest and added politely, "You have an absolutely splendid church here for such a remote part of our glorious land."

"Indeed, I was just saying to your charming sister..."

"Excuse me for interrupting, sir." A soldier walked up the aisle.

"What is it, my man?" the priest asked.

"There has been an incident at the barracks and your presence is requested there," the soldier explained.

"Well, is it so urgent that I should close up the church or is it a simple issue that can be dealt with tomorrow?"

"I'm afraid it is that urgent."

"Then we must be on our way, Elizabeth, and allow you to see to your duties." Willoughby held an arm out for Beth. She gracefully stepped from the aisle. Willoughby carried his bag in his other hand.

The vicar turned to speak to them, then hesitated as he saw the splintered wood of one of the pews where the man had been thrown down.

"Is nowhere sacred these days?" He shook his head.

Willoughby sympathised with the sentiment, before walking Beth outside into the cool of the evening.

They blended into the crowds of milling people as soon as possible, walking boldly past a group of soldiers who had just left an inn. Willoughby led Beth straight into one opposite.

Beth tugged his sleeve. "Where did the cane come from? It weren't in the bag for sure."

"Did you snoop?" he asked.

"No! I wouldn't do that to you, Mr James, not through your stuff — honest."

"I believe you."

"You do?" Her eyes were wide.

Had no one trusted her before? he wondered briefly. "It is special. It collapses. Come in here." He led her into a tall and narrow hotel with a fashionable bay window and a serving counter within. "Has someone escaped from gaol or something? There seems to be a lot of soldiers scurrying around the alleyways and at this hour of the day," he remarked to the landlord brightly.

"No, nothing so common. They're searching for a murdering priest and a stranger dressed as a soldier," replied the innkeeper.

"Really, well the priest should stand out easily enough amongst the crowd, but the soldier … it will be like seeking a needle in a haystack!"

The landlord nodded.

"Have you two rooms available that would be suitable for my sister and myself?" Willoughby enquired, and pulled his purse from his coat pocket.

The man reached down and found two keys. "Yes, I should say so. Would rooms that are next to each other do?" he asked and smiled at Beth. "How long do you wish to stay, sir?"

"One night will be sufficient." Willoughby looked around the narrow room, dark and airless as it was, not able to see much in the corners of the gloom.

"It can get a little lively later, although I do keep a respectable inn. So would you want your meals fetching up?"

"I think it would be much more suitable if we dined upstairs." Willoughby placed some coins in the man's hand. "Please see that we are not disturbed."

"Oh, aye, sir." He chuckled. "I'll do that, not to worry." The man took Willoughby's bag up the stairs and Beth followed with Willoughby close behind her.

Beth had noted the look that passed between the two men as he exchanged the money, but she let it wash over her without comment if it meant they would be left safe and alone. Strange, Beth thought, to wonder that even in her new clothes, in here, an inn, people might see her for what she was: a common whore. Had what had happened to her in the past few months of her life left a visible stain upon her that could not be washed off?

# Chapter 12

Beth entered the small, narrow bedchamber. The innkeeper placed Willoughby's bag on top of the bed, which was nestled against a wooden panelled wall. Between the bed and the panelled wall stood a small table on which a jug of water had been placed. Luxury! thought Beth. She had found paradise.

"Your brother will be just next door, miss," the man said. "You settle yourself in and I'll have a meal sent up in about ... an hour?" He turned, raising an eyebrow as if to ask if that would be sufficient time.

"That would be most agreeable," Willoughby answered and smiled at the man.

The door closed behind them and Beth stared blankly out of the window at the ramshackle display of red pantiled roofs opposite. Here she could not see the country or the open sea; instead she looked upon a lonely gull that landed on the chimney stack in front of her small window, making a keen racket with its desperate call.

The voices from the corridor ceased and she heard Willoughby close his door. In the next moment there was a faint tap on the cedar panel.

"Come in," she said hesitantly. She had felt safe with the man who had rescued her from the inn, but dressed as a fashionable gentleman he appeared almost rakish, definitely handsome, confident; but how did she know if he was still at all honourable? Did she care? If he asked her to go to his bed, she would, she knew it and no doubt he did too. Was that why he had her scrubbed raw? After Wilkes, Willoughby would be like embracing heaven after experiencing hell. He was kind to her. She was sure he would make a fine lover. Beth thought he would look more at home in the company of a fine lady in a spectacular carriage like the one that had passed them by at the moor inn than with the likes of her. Why was she even thinking like this? She had sworn never to let another wretch touch her, but Willoughby was no mere wretch.

Willoughby slid the panel slowly back along a runner. It was obviously well used as it made little sound. Its path was smooth and unhindered. They stood for a moment staring at each other across the open space, not three feet separated them, each standing in front of their own bed. It seemed strange to him, yet at the same time, the most natural thing in the world was to share his dilemma with this young woman who was really no more than a stranger, a lost soul, and it would appear his new companion. They both now needed the other.

"You are a very appealing young lady, Beth. Thank you for being in the right place, when I needed you," Willoughby said softly and tossed his hat and cane onto the bed behind him.

"Thank you for the compliment, and let me return it, whatever and whoever you is ... sir. You're my sort of gent. You is running from trouble. It seems that you are in more bother than me. That takes some doing." She smiled at him.

Willoughby glanced out of the window, but was careful to stand to the side, unseen from the searching eyes below. He definitely needed Beth, and that, he also realised, was all that mattered to her at that precise moment. He crossed over the line between them and held her hands in his. "I will make all this right, I promise you, and I know that at this moment I must appear to be like one of the biggest rogues you have ever met, but please find it in your heart, Beth, to trust me still." He watched her eyes fill with humour. She was so easy to read, she did not have the guile of a minx, but an open heart, beguiling and child-like, despite what fate had thrown across her path to deal with.

"You a rogue? That's a fine notion. You may have floored Wilkes, and you're not what you pretends to be, brother Will, but a rogue you ain't! I've met them for real, I don't have to pretend to be what I'm not with you, so why not share that honesty with me?" Beth hesitated for a moment. "If I hadn't placed my trust firmly in you, you would not now be standing here."

He carefully slipped his hands from her.

"You have yet to truly discover who and what you are or want to be, Beth. This is your new start. No past exists for you. Forget it as soon as you are able and decide who you will be from this day forwards."

"Tell me first, before I decide to be a Lady to a grand Lord, why a priest left me and now I am sharing lodgings with me 'brother'?"

He looked at the floor and clenched his fists tightly.

Beth persisted. "I think you owe me an explanation. It's obvious you have the soldiers combing the town for you. Who and what are you, Mr James?" Beth stood directly in front of him. She reached up and placed her hand gently on his cheek and turned his head to face her. Responding to her gentle touch, Willoughby raised his hand to hers, but did not remove it. "I want to help you."

"You are very sweet, but I am a dangerous person to know. I need to leave here early in the morning and once we have made our way to Ebton and you are found a home, I shall be out of your life, and then you shall be safe once more." Willoughby gestured that she should sit down on the bed and be in more comfort. He stepped as far away from her as he could, which was by the cedar panel.

"You're not staying in Ebton with me?" Beth sat down.

"No, I shall be moving around this coast."

"Why?" Beth stared at him and he looked for a moment as if he would say more, but something was preventing him. "At least tell me if you are a true priest and what happened at the barracks. It's obvious that whatever you is up to, I should be a part of it, yet still you fight fate and try to cast me off."

"I don't want you hurt anymore," Willoughby explained.

"Then stick with me. You can't keep me from danger. Believe me, I manage to find it all by myself."

He shook his head at her, amazed how her simple logic was starting to make sense to him. "I was never ordained."

"Did you floor someone in anger and get kicked out of school?" Her eyes sparkled with mischief.

"Not quite. I opted to leave. My family intended that I follow the tradition and become a fully-fledged priest and work at my vocation until I became a bishop. However, I did not. So I chose a different path."

"And what path do you choose now?" Beth asked.

"I wanted to be a soldier, but it was my older brother who had that option. My father's estate had already passed into the care of his brother, and so Charles was destined to fight for his king and family honour. The irony is that he wanted to be in the church; he would have made a good future of it and I would have made a damn good officer." There was passion in his words and, as he raised his hand to stress his point, the scar on his wrist became visible.

"It looks like you took up your first choice of fighting anyway," Beth commented and moved his hand upward, pointing to the scar. "You have estates. You is a real gentleman then."

"I chose a path of honour and duty," he said in explanation, and then shrugged as if dismissing it. He allowed his hand to stay. "I have said too much already, Beth."

"So how are you to tell your family that you are now being hunted for murder?"

"That is one of my dilemmas because I cannot involve them in any of this. I am on my own here and as far as anyone is concerned I have no position, family or friends." He looked out of the window and fell silent for a moment until a fleeting smile crossed his face once more. "I have blood on my hands and hatred in my heart and they are deeply ignoble traits for any man, let alone a man of God, so I shall definitely never be a priest."

"Congratulations, Willoughby, you're a man, not a bloody saint!" Beth was not laughing. "You have a friend who can and will help you. You got me!"

Willoughby looked at her. "Why have you not asked me if I killed the major? You did not even look surprised when I changed my apparel. You were most willing to fall in with my plans and that was before you knew the soldiers were looking for me, Beth. Why so?"

"When I was in the church I decided to explore the gallery. I heard two men talking below in them pews. One was a soldier, the other looked like Spratt, and sounded like him also ... he was paying him for 'finishing off' the major. He was supposed to find a list on him, but said a priest had arrived and he had had to leave sooner than expected." Willoughby listened to her, hanging on her every word. This woman, the burden he thought he would carry with him, was as if placed in his path to help him sort out the mess he had found himself in. "It must have been poison because he'd hoped the priest had drunk it too. He pushed the man into one of the pews, which was how the door got broken. Then he asked if you were local and when the man said no, he asked if you had yellow hair." Beth looked down at her lap. "He thwacked him real hard. I bet his nose is broader now than it was this morning. For a few awful moments I feared you might be dead also. I was recovering your bag when you came in. I was so pleased to see you that I accepted whatever you said, so long as we could escape before Spratt returned. I could go to the soldiers and tell them what I heard, but you know they aren't going to believe me, Willoughby. Spratt knew it was you from the description. He realised he'd seen you on the moor road. He'll be after you too now and he has eyes everywhere. You're in deep trouble."

"Can you tell me anything more about the soldier?"

Beth hesitated.

"Anything, Beth, it could mean the difference between life and death; yours as well as mine." He knelt on the floor before her and held her shoulders firmly but gently.

"He has a bloody nose, but beyond that...."

Willoughby sat back on his haunches. "Thank you, Beth."

A knock on the door made Beth stand up guiltily; Willoughby toppled backwards and a stranger's voice announced, "Dinner, ma'am."

Willoughby rolled full circle and stood up in his own room beyond the safety of the runner. He bowed with grace and pulled the panel quietly back to form a solid barrier. Beth admired the athletic way he moved — she admired much about Willoughby.

"Please bring it in." Beth opened the door.

A maid entered, furtively looking around. Beth closed the door behind her as she left and locked it.

She heard Willoughby do the same and then it was her turn to slide back the panel.

"Should we dine together, sir?" she asked, as she then sat on her bed with the tray placed on her lap.

"An excellent idea, Miss Elizabeth." He brought his tray through and they sat side by side enjoying the food, both deep in thought.

Once their meal was finished, the two new friends looked at each other with full stomachs and a relaxed manner.

"Miss Elizabeth, I like the sound of that."

"It suits the new you," he admitted.

"Willoughby, do you have a sharp knife?" Beth asked, and she carefully placed half of her tea in a dish on the side table.

"Yes, but why do you need one?"

She ran her fingers through his hair, and his eyes sparkled with each stroke of her hand. "I fear you need a shorter more fashionable haircut, much as it grieves me to cut off such handsome locks."

"You promise you won't slip?" he quipped.

"I promise."

For the next half an hour Beth cut short his hair. She was careful that each lock was collected and wrapped in a kerchief as she did not want to leave a trace of what they had done. One lock quickly tied by a long strand found itself secreted into her pocket. It was a momentary whim, but it made her heart feel warm to know it was there.

Once she had finished she then combed the now strong tea through it, to darken its hue.

"This feels extremely odd." He looked at himself in the looking glass and shook his head. "The things I do for King and country," he muttered to himself, then realised what he had said, as Beth stared enquiringly back at him, eyebrows raised. "Time for bed! We have an early start tomorrow and neither of us has been able to get a good rest." He quickly moved the table he had been seated on back to its position by the window. "It appears our water is not to be brought... Thank you," he said, and took the knife from her hand, before disappearing behind the cedar panel.

Beth gazed thoughtfully at the wall. "Good night," she said and lay down on her own bed, fully clothed, repeating his words, "For King and country, eh?"

# Chapter 13

Willoughby looked out at a darkening sky. He held his father's wallet in his hand. Seating himself by the table, he stroked at the wrap-around leather. The old skin bore the white marks of the sea salt, yet was still quite supple, so it had dried out naturally; except for the charred edge where it had touched flames, it was as it would have been when it was tucked safely next to his father's body. With a broken tie fastening dangling from its seam, he held it almost with reverence because it had rested against his father's beating chest when his heart was full of life. Willoughby carefully unrolled it to reveal whatever secrets lay within. The charred edge seemed as an insult to its precarious survival of his father's fall and death. It had escaped one tragedy, only to have nearly perished into a fire's flames — that was another mystery — when and how had it been burnt?

Inside there was a piece of newsprint. This had, Willoughby realised, been included at a later time as it was the obituary of his father's death.

*Joshua Willoughby Rossington, Esq.*
*It is in sadness we have to report the demise of Mr Rossington. The gentleman's body was discovered washed up upon the beach at the small fishing village of Ebton, having fallen to his death from the treacherous path skirting the headland of Stangcliffe. Mr Rossington was a man of standing, Oxbridge educated, a scholar who was studying the local geology. Although brave in the extreme, he defied the hazardous terrain and severe weather conditions accustomed to this coastline in order to prosecute his task. It is with regret that we must announce he perished along with the samples he so carefully collected...*

Willoughby placed this to the side, as he had seen it before. The words — the lies — were etched on his heart. Willoughby swallowed back raw emotions, as the description did not fit the man he knew. It was a mockery to his father's intelligence and dedicated life of service. No more than a fog created to obscure a murder. Even in death, he had done his duty.

Willoughby then slipped out a more delicate piece of paper. The marks upon it were erratic. On one side he could just make out a sketch of the rocky cliffs of the coast. It was a hastily drawn map of the coastline. On the other, letters were roughly scribbled.

He opened it carefully. He was sure that the sketch was of a specific section of the coast. It was not part of a final message, but had been the reason perhaps that the paper had been within the man's pocket at the time. It may give the location that his father was studying, or could have been part of his cover as he was supposed to be surveying the area.

The letters were still mostly legible, some were missing — possibly the scribbling of a desperate man, one in a hurry, shaky of hand — hurt, perhaps. Willoughby tried to still the pain such thoughts brought to him. This was his father's last chance to speak to him. He felt the agonised cry for help. His eyes watered despite his best efforts to concentrate on the issue of the murder and not his own devastation.

Willoughby looked up through the small window and stared out at the now darkened sky. If God was there, He had never answered that one question that every bereaved person wanted to shout out: 'Why?' But this was a man-made murder and not divine intervention, so it fell to a man to unravel the truth. Good had been slain by evil and now he was to address the balance and bring his father justice.

Willoughby breathed deeply, calming his troubled mind, and then returned to task. He lit a second lamp to cast as much light as he could and studied the sketch. It was faded, yet on the rugged cliffs he could make out lines that looked possibly like tracks going down to the shore. They looked to be more than footpaths. Fires burned on the land and what could have been buildings had faded away, leaving an ethereal presence. Why?

He ran his fingers through his newly cut hair. It felt strange, yet he could see the sense in it. Think! Husk had said that Joshua had taken to walking near the alum works further along the coast. Had he another reason to go there?

Willoughby looked at the scrawled desperate words. He had been trying to get a message to Nathaniel. One name was clear 'Simon...' Then the writing faded. 'In Mother I'... but then the last word melted into an illegible line. Lastly, at the edge as if his words were falling off the paper were the compass bearings 'N to S', then nothing. He stared at it. Who was Simon? Looking at the list retrieved from Major Husk, he could not see Simon mentioned. There was his contact in Ebton, Reverend Burdon, Mr R Ingham, and Oberon Spratt. No mention of a Simon. Willoughby stared at the name Burdon. Did this mean he too had been under suspicion?

He thought more about the words on the note. Why Mother? Why north to south? Why not the other way around? If that was the trade route, it bore no great revelation. He was missing something, but could not grasp what it was. Tired and weary from the day's events he extinguished the lamps and pulled off his boots. He would remain clothed in case of action as there was still a heavy presence of soldiers in the streets below.

Tomorrow he would take Beth away from Whitby and travel north, keeping as near as they could to the coastal route. Beth was going to have the opportunity to see even more of the sea as they made their way to Upthorpe Hall, the home of the Inghams, owners of a fine coach and the alum mines. Beth could be a spy for him whilst he left her somewhere safe, using her quick wit to look inside their home. Would Beth trust him? She had no choice. What other options did life hold for such a downtrodden beauty?

Willoughby closed his eyes for some much needed rest; happier visions of his father returned to him, filled his thoughts as he began to drift off to sleep, just as the cry outside went up.

Willoughby heard noises coming from below amidst much commotion. He left his room and edged along the narrow hall to the stairs. Here he listened from the top of the stairwell to the innkeeper's conversations with worried locals until he could ascertain what had happened. News was soon brought in from the street that a body of a soldier had been dragged out of the harbour.

The innkeeper was dismissive. "What, drunk out of his wits, eh, been visiting a harbour side doxy, no doubt."

"No, Silas, not this one. He might have stumbled in, but only because he had a knife wound in his back. I tell you it's a bad business this."

Willoughby strained to listen, guessing that the dead man was the makeshift soldier with the scuffed boots, the man who had poisoned the major. If he had been murdered, then someone was covering their tracks. His key suspect would now be Mr Oberon Spratt.

He returned to his room, checking that Beth had not heard the disturbance. She was nestled in the bed, sleeping soundly.

Willoughby realised he would be Spratt's next target, and Beth, if he had seen her. He flopped on his bed, imagining what his Uncle Nathaniel would make of the mess he was now in. He was both the hunter and the hunted.

After a fitful sleep, Willoughby refreshed himself and arose early and made his way down the rickety wooden staircase. The innkeeper was up early, organising the maids and stores. "Sleep well, sir?"

"Excellently, thank you. Tell me, where can I purchase the use of a gig? We wish to explore the coast a little."

"Sir, this is a dangerous coast, particularly after last night's murder, and the roads are not so smooth."

"Murder?" Willoughby repeated. "You mean there was a murder … here … yesterday?"

"Aye, a soldier, knifed in the back and tossed into the Esk."

"I hope they caught the culprit." Willoughby was no actor, but he feigned an expression of utter disgust and dismay.

"I'm afraid not, but don't you worry any, they will." The innkeeper leaned over to him. "There can't be too many places where a murdering priest can hide."

"A priest!" Willoughby exclaimed.

"Aye, this is a close community. People have eyes and ears." He winked at him and Willoughby nodded. "He ain't no man of God. He be hiding behind God's garments. He'll go to hell for that and soon I reckon."

"Look." Willoughby fidgeted a little nervously, acting like a fop, as if the news had unnerved him grievously. "My sister, you understand, would be shocked and dismayed by such unpleasantness. Could you send your man to fetch the gig for me, if I give you the money for your services? Then I should not have to leave her on her own."

The man, sensing a profit was to be made, nodded agreeably. "Very wise, sir. I'm sure we can negotiate a fair price for you."

"Of course, of course... I shall need two blankets and hot bricks for the journey. Damn cold place this is, at this time of year. We may decide to return south." Willoughby anxiously completed his deal and arranged for a light meal for them both whilst they waited. He knew the innkeeper thought he was a coward, who at the mention of a murderer on the loose had sought to evacuate the town, but that was exactly his intention.

He returned to his room. Slowly he slid back the cedar panel and stood watching Beth for a few moments as she lay on the bed blissfully asleep, untroubled. But time was precious and if he was not going to be found and hanged for two murders he had not committed, they had to be on their way. 'For King and country' he repeated in his mind as he gently stroked her cheek.

Beth felt Willoughby's finger gently touch her skin. It was a warm, comforting sensation. Her half sleep drifted away as she became more conscious of the soft touch. Slowly, she opened her eyes to the early morning light. The curtain had been drawn back and Willoughby's handsome face smiled down at her.

She opened her mouth to speak to him, but he placed a finger to her lips. His voice was no more than a whisper. "We need to leave here as soon as possible. It isn't safe to stay any longer. I meant only to wake you gently from your slumber in case you had forgotten where you were."

"It is the most pleasant way I have ever been woken that I can remember. You are excused." Beth's voice was equally hushed. Her eyes, still heavy with sleep, seemed to be taking in every aspect of his features.

Willoughby smiled at her and realised her face had tilted to his. She had glanced at his mouth as if considering whether to invite a kiss. He was surprised that he felt like responding. He quickly stood up. "We have little enough time, I'm afraid. It is essential that we should hurry ... please."

She watched his back as he walked away, sliding the panel until it was closed behind him. She wanted to take the look of concern from his face by telling him that all would be well, like he had unwittingly done for her, but how could she when it could be a lie? As she stared out of her small window and across the roof tops she tidied her hair as quickly as she could. It was not something she had needed to do for some time, but hoped she had made a tolerable attempt at looking respectable. Her stomach felt most peculiar — it fluttered anxiously.

Beth was about to leave this town with a man, a stranger who masqueraded as her brother, just as he had 'masqueraded as a priest', possibly, she thought, remembering his words, for 'King and country'. Could he be a sort of soldier himself? Or, more likely a revenue officer? She stared at the door. That would be funny, her careering around with a revenue man, then her face fell into a look of dread — Spratt wouldn't find it so. What sort of person lived a life of so many lies, yet still had honour? He hadn't killed the major, that she knew for sure, but why had he not gone to the authorities? Beth followed her heart as her head was too confused by the speed of recent events. Besides, her intuition told her Willoughby was a good man, who needed her as much as she needed him, at least until they reached Ebton. Beth liked the idea of being needed. She'd been wanted, like a possession, but to be needed, that made her feel special. An image of Spratt appeared in her mind; she would stay with Willoughby as long as she could until they were both safe. He needed someone to look out for him. Whatever he was, he was too soft to survive in Spratt's world.

There was a faint knock on the door. Beth opened it warily. The small maid held a plate in one hand, and a small tankard in the other.

"Food, ma'am," she said and dipped slightly.

Beth took the plate and ale from her and nodded.

Beth ate as quickly as she could and then slowly opened the panel wide with gloved hand. "I'm ready," she said brightly and smiled at Willoughby who had been sitting studying a scrap of paper.

"Good." He quickly put it safely away. "Stay with me," he told her.

"Yes, brother Willoughby," she answered sweetly and then smiled at him a little nervously.

"We shall leave. There is a gig waiting outside. I am sorry it will not be that comfortable, but it will allow us to travel on the smaller roads, rutted though they will be." Willoughby leaned forward, and for a moment, she believed he was going to kiss her cheek.

She stood motionless and waited, without flinching. However, he picked up his bag from the floor by the panel and straightened up again. Willoughby stepped back so that she could walk ahead of him, but she saw the humour in his eyes. He had realised her misunderstanding. Beth walked swiftly out of the room; her body was swept by an unfamiliar wave of emotion — anticipation. She had never been tenderly caressed, and she found herself imagining what Willoughby's touch would feel like against her skin and wishing one day soon she could find out. The journey was going to be a trial for her in a very new way; that was if they survived and escaped from their pursuers.

"Stay here a moment, Elizabeth." Willoughby tapped her arm once they had reached the downstairs room. "I want to make sure it is safe before you go outside." He patted her on the shoulder. "Don't worry, I won't be long."

Beth watched him leave. When he called her 'Elizabeth' her heartbeat quickened. It was as if she was a new person. In such a short time he had given her everything, a life, and taken nothing in return. Beth swore she would look after him.

She stared around the dark panelled interior of the inn, the air still thick with the smell of smoke and ale from the night before. The gig was just visible through the small panel of the window and, for the first time that she could remember, prayed that they would get away safely and that it would not rain today. Then a thought crossed her mind: What if Ebton was more than a day's journey away? She felt herself tremble slightly, not knowing why. The stories of 'ill omens' and 'creatures of the moor' flooded her mind.

Outside, Beth was helped up into the gig. The air was bracing as gulls kwaarked up above. Already the place was a cacophony of noise with the sounds from the busy shipyards, waves crashing against headland and harbour, birds screeching overhead and carts clattering over cobbled streets. Willoughby flicked the reins and moved the horse onwards. It trotted up the steep bank, and Beth held on to Willoughby's arm tightly. Once safely at the crown of the hill, he looked back across the harbour to the abbey ruins on the cliff at the far side of the town.

"We can still find work for you where you will be safe," Willoughby said gently. "You don't have to become involved in my mess, Beth. I will give you the choice, but I would ask you to tell me what you know of Spratt before we parted."

"No need, Mr Willoughby, I think it is too late. It appears we are both involved in a right mess. I ain't going nowhere."

Willoughby turned his attention to the road ahead as he sped them on their way.

# Chapter 14

With the moors on their left and the rugged cliff tops and bays to the right, Beth and Willoughby set off on what looked to be little more than a well-used track. This was the road which would eventually lead them to the fishing village of Ebton.

"This isn't as good as the York road, is it?" Beth commented as she looked around at a group of motley looking sheep that were idly ambling across the trackway ahead. "Perhaps we should not be here."

"Here is where we need to be. Perhaps you should tell me all you know about Spratt and if you have heard anything about the Inghams who own Upthorpe Hall."

"Perhaps you should've left me in Whitby for Spratt to feed me to the fishes if that's where you're going to dump me." She looked at him; there was always humour and a challenge in those eyes.

"I asked you for information. You will come with me on this journey as far as the vicarage at Ebton; from there we shall make new plans." Willoughby held the reins loosely in one hand as they made slow progress up the track. If they were followed or chased they would be no better than sitting ducks. However, he was now openly travelling, a gentleman and with his sister, not a single priest hiding in fear of his life.

"Mrs Ingham is a bad tempered bitch if ever there was one. She comes to York for assemblies and 'assignations'. Thinks she is a true lady and she ain't. I knows it cos I heard Jacob talking about how he'd driven her once and the coach lost a wheel and she hit him with her crop. He has a scar on the back of his neck where the edge cut him."

Willoughby looked at her incredulously. "Do you know what that word means — assignations?"

"Aye, posh way of being tupped with expensive gents like yourself." Her defiant look met Willoughby's impassive one, as he refused to be drawn by her attempts to shock him. "Wilkes used to drink with one of her maids who came to the inn when her ladyship was in town. One day, she had a black eye like the best of them that Wilkes can give. Only she got it simply for not answering her ladyship proper in front of her friend. I won't be working for that woman, for sure. I'd not survive the week without being cuffed."

"You won't have to, Beth. Tell me, this servant, why was she with Wilkes?" Willoughby asked.

"She always comes to the inn when her ladyship is in town."

"You said that, but was there a reason?"

Beth shrugged and looked around her. "How would I know?"

"Because, Beth, you never know when to stop listening, do you?"

"Never heard them say anything more than normal gossip." She fell silent, but Willoughby was not convinced.

"This is a remote part of the country, Beth, and I have chosen to take a road which is not the main coach route, but we should be able to travel some way along it unseen and undisturbed."

"That could be dangerous enough by itself, Mr James, Reverend Mr Willoughby, sir, or whoever you really are." Beth stared at him.

He side-glanced at her but remained silent.

"I dread to think what folk would be thinking," Beth continued unperturbed. She was pushing for Willoughby to tell her the truth. "You leave me with your bag and then they're combing the town hunting for a murdering priest. So tell me, what is your real name and why are you here?" She still had her hand cupped around his elbow. "Are you a real gentleman, or do you pretend that too?"

Willoughby laughed. "You wish me to answer all those questions at once or one question at a time?"

"Any way you like, but the honest truth for once would be nice, seeing as I have given away my reputation to help save your life," she said straight faced, but could not hold the expression, and chuckled.

"Your reputation, I believe, was already in shreds. However, I do appreciate your recent help. Would you believe me if I told you that the less you know about me the better it will be for you? I have a dull past and an uncertain future, Beth."

"Don't we all?"

Willoughby stared straight ahead as they came over a brow of a hill and a different landscape was revealed to them. On the horizon were fires rising high into the sky and all was a mass of activity. He realised that they were heading towards the alum works, recognising them from his father's sketch.

"Bloody hell — and I mean just that. They look like the fires of hell itself!"

"How would you know that?" Willoughby smiled at her. "They are just fires."

Her expression changed to a sombre look. "I should do, I've been there often enough." She sniffed and stared out at the open sea.

Willoughby shook his head and then studied the land in front of him. "I was born in Kent. There, I have answered one of your questions, now you answer one of mine." He scanned the country around them as they travelled along. "What do you really know about Oberon Spratt?"

"Just what everyone else does about him. He mixes, he trades, he murders by the hands of others and no one knows where he lays his head on a night unless he appears at your door. No one knows where his contacts come from and no one asks him anything. He moves around like a ghost in the night, unseen, quick, and has been said to have been seen in three inns at the same time in different places. He has powers. Everyone gets paid for doing their part, and they keep their mouths shut or he closes them permanently."

"How convenient for him. But perhaps you have answered one question. That hat of his stands out in a crowd. It isn't him that is seen in three places, but the hat — or copies of it."

"Where are we going?"

"To innocently ask directions from the people within that house over there." He pointed towards a large, bleak stone building that had pride of place on the raised ground. The stable block behind it was almost as grand in its modern design as the house itself. Young trees had been planted to act as a screen between it and the gales that would sweep across this part of the land. It faced away from the distant alum works. As the gig pulled up in front of the gates of a long drive, Willoughby looked down at Beth. "Do you know who owns this property?"

"No. Should I?" Beth stared at it and shrugged her shoulders. A movement caught her eye. Being prepared at the seaward side of the house was a carriage, unmistakable in its design and grandeur, the same initials adorning its side as seen at the inn in Whitby.

"Yes, yes I do! It's that bloody woman … Ingham, and you've brought me to her house, you said you wouldn't — you lied! Do you want us both dead? If the maid sees me she'll tell Wilkes for sure."

"No, I don't want us dead, but I need to find out something and I can only do that by visiting. Her husband owns the alum works."

"So? I could have told you that before you brought us here. Anyway you're wrong, he owns half. Some London gent owns the other half. Ingham owns the boats that transport the alum to London and brings back boat loads of piss to complete the process," Beth said smugly, and laughed as Willoughby's eyes lit up with humour. "They use it to make dye."

Willoughby's expression changed abruptly. "How do you know all this?" he asked.

"I overheard a conversation between Wilkes and the maid saying as when the piss was due to arrive. They were very annoyed when a shipment was lost to a storm off Whitby."

"Pity the fish!"

"Some souls were lost in it, I believe. What a way to go, dying for a piss!" she chuckled.

# Chapter 15

Willoughby manoeuvred the gig behind the line of trees. Before he had the chance to speak to her, Beth jumped down.

"Did I tell you to alight?" he asked.

"No, and you didn't tell me to get off either, but I ain't going to that house, Mr Willoughby. I'd rather jump from the cliff than let Spratt get his hands on me, and if I goes in there, either him or Wilkes, or both, will know it in double-quick time and then that's me done for!"

Willoughby felt himself flinch as she referred to jumping off a cliff. "Never say you will even consider such a thing, even to merely stress one of your points." He leaned forward to speak. "Do you think I would lumber myself with your presence only to give your life up to them?"

Beth stared at him dumbfounded. She thought he had complimented her, said she was of some importance, but was not sure.

"Beth, walk down to the wall that skirts the edge of the coast there, stay out of sight of the inn below, and nestle against it. Stay in shelter there, so that when I return I can find you easily enough. Don't go wandering off on your own; this time I shall not detour to find you. Lost will remain lost — clear?"

"Why don't I stay in the trees?"

"Because then you would be found by anyone approaching or leaving the house."

He ignored her scowl and manoeuvred the gig along the avenue into the drive. Willoughby felt peculiarly uneasy as he approached the austere building in silence. Was this man the reason his father had visited the alum works? Were they

126

involved in the downfall of his father's investigation? He thought it more and more likely.

Beth did as she was told, but sulked as she ran down to the wall and walked along, following a lonely track. The land fell away as the line of cliffs dipped down on the seaward side. The inn ahead may one day fall itself, she thought, as it lay precariously low to the edge. Looking out at the sea, she ventured further than she had been meant to as the view was magnificent. It seemed to stretch forever and the ships that went up and down it fascinated her. The sense of freedom that swept through her mind made her feel alive in a way she had never known. In her excitement she ran along the length of the wall, smiling, skipping like a child, playing and enjoying being able to. No one to shout her name angrily, no fist to threaten, no hand to slap and no ... no lying down for a brute when he wished it so. Beth stopped suddenly when her hat was nearly blown away.

She paused to catch her breath and had just decided to turn around, thinking it was time she should amble back to where Willoughby had told her to hide, when she heard voices which surprised her, as she could not see anyone. She craned her neck to see over the wall but there was only overgrown land that sloped away abruptly to the sea below. Beth became very aware of something not being quite right, a strange feeling that she was not alone, as if she was being watched. She turned around slowly. Two local fishermen were standing there, staring at her. She had not seen them approach. They were like phantoms appearing out of thin air.

"Well it ain't a mermaid," said one carrying a walking stick.

"Nope, I've seen 'em when I've been whaling and they don't wear bonnets. Nor have legs what run around the countryside," said the other.

"Greetings, gents," Beth said brightly, "I was just making my way down to yonder inn from the big house and didn't realise how far it was." Beth paused because she had glanced a few yards further on and realised these men had come out of a camouflaged hole in the wall. She could hazard a guess that they had been stashing or retrieving smuggled goods and she had walked straight into them. Willoughby, bloody Willoughby, had told her to come here. Stay by the wall, he'd said. What the hell did the stupid non-priest know of anything? He needed her to keep him alive, but he could yet be the death of her. If she'd stayed in the trees she'd have been safe. She'd have hidden from anyone coming or going. He had no bloody sense. "I best get back before Mrs Ingham returns. Excuse me, gents." She started to walk along by the wall. One of them stepped in front of her. Beth looked up at him, as if surprised. "Is there a problem, sir?"

"Aye, there is. You said as you were going to yonder inn. Well, we'll help you on your way." In one swift move, he bent down and swung her over his shoulder.

Beth started screaming and kicking. His friend whacked her rump hard with the walking stick and she yelped. "Quiet or I'll throw you down there!" He used the stick to point to the sea, beyond the cliff edge.

She settled, still cursing quietly to herself. Where was her freedom now?

"Finish off here, and I'll take this ragamuffin to the inn."

"Aye, lock her up in the cellar 'til he comes. He'll know what to do with her."

Beth felt the grip around her tighten as she was carried off. Tears of frustration welled up in her eyes. Now it was her who needed Willoughby again. Why, she wondered, did every man she ever met let her down or treat her like dirt? As she watched her lovely hat roll along the ground, she sobbed.

Willoughby slowed the vehicle to a halt outside the colonnaded entrance of the house. He studied its grandeur and, despite the initial bleak appearance, he realised it was actually far more opulent than he had thought. From here he had a clear view across the bay. The power of the sea was wild and breathtaking, in a way that the sheltered splendour of the landscaped gardens of his country estate could never be. One was safe, artificial, controlled, although appreciated, whilst this estate was open, exposed, atmospheric and beyond human interference — a beautiful yet dangerous place.

The double doors of the house were opened by a liveried footman, and then the lady of the house appeared, already attired in an emerald green velvet travelling coat, with matching hat. She stepped out; her beauty close to was quite stunning. He glanced at her eyes and wished he could read into her thoughts; what secrets she could tell him.

Had his father been drawn to her beguiling ways? Could it have led to an affair? The lady's face in the first instance showed surprise, almost annoyance, when she realised it was not her own vehicle that had arrived to collect her but one of a stranger. She stared at Willoughby for a moment, her eyes taking in his full frame.

"You must excuse me, please, Mrs Ingham."

"Must I?" she said briskly. She came forward, descending a step to focus her attention fully on Willoughby's face. Her demeanour changed completely to one of geniality itself. "Well it appears I must," she mused.

"Please," Willoughby said, "I was making my way north when I saw your wonderful home and wondered if it would be possible to meet with Mr Ingham, in person, if he is at home today?"

Her charm seemed to have left her fleetingly. "Mr Ingham is in Newcastle this week."

"I am sorry to have missed him."

"We shall leave your card on his desk for his return."

Willoughby patted his pocket. "I am afraid that I have been most remiss and I have no card to offer. However, I shall pass by again when I too return in a week's time and see if he is at home then."

"Sir, you talk like a gentleman. Have you no coach? Why travel in such a humble fashion as a hired vehicle?"

"These roads, ma'am, are not designed for fine coaches, and I wish to explore this rugged coast a little before returning in comfort to my estate."

"Your name, sir?"

"James," he replied. "Mr James."

"Unfortunately, I have an appointment to attend and cannot therefore share my hospitality with you." The lady's voice had lost some of its sharpness, but she seemed anxious to be on her way as her own coach appeared.

"Then I shall not inconvenience you any further." Willoughby stepped down from the gig, leaving the footman holding the reins, and approached the lady.

She seemed to hold herself aloof as she breathed in and poised herself. He looked into her seductive eyes; they were worldly, knowing, and they stared back at his face with a growing sense of recognition. He removed his hat. Willoughby was well aware that he carried the looks of his father. He saw it often enough in the portraits in their family home.

"It has been a pleasure to meet you, in person. I shall return at a more convenient time to both of us, Mrs Ingham." He bowed.

It was possible that she was his father's mistress. He felt a fleeting feeling of regret for his poor plain mother who, lovely as she was in character, could never have competed with this 'lady' in beauty or guile. If her husband was the man he sought then she may hold a key to his undoing. He returned to the gig. He could not go to his uncle with whims; he needed proof.

Willoughby climbed back onto the gig and flicked the horse's rear with the reins, moving swiftly off. He glanced back over his shoulder; she was standing like a statue, motionless, as she stared back until he departed. She would know he was his father's son. Now he would retrieve Beth quickly and they would follow her and find out who she would tell. She would run, of that he was sure. A woman like her had too much to lose, but it also meant his own identity would become known and that Nathaniel had forbidden him to divulge.

He trotted the horse away from the avenue and along the cliff path back towards the alum works, looking for Beth along the wall. There was no sign of her. "Damn that girl!" he swore. Had he not told her to stay by the wall? He was trying to control his anger. He had told her there was no time for him to go looking for her should she roam, yet she had still disobeyed him.

From the quarry down to the shore was a mass of activity as the long process of producing the alum perpetually continued as it had done over the centuries. Pack horses took the heavy sacks of pure alum down the steep ramps to the beach where the large-wheeled red and green carts waited to unload and load the flat-bottomed boats that had entered on the tide.

He recognised the scene from his father's sketch, but where had the damn wench gone, and had he the heart of a true spy to abandon her to her fate and continue alone?

# Chapter 16

Willoughby looked at the road that bypassed the main workings of the alum factories. There was a village there to house the mine workers. He was not shocked at the state of the people's homes; he had seen the hardship of poverty.

It was so far removed from life at Upthorpe Hall, that it did not seem possible that two such different worlds co-existed; one providing luxury for the other. Willoughby had read something of the lengthy process before coming to the region. The alum had to be mined, boiled and separated from the mother liquor. What was it … the mother liquor, '*Mother I*' or maybe 'L'?" Had he remembered just enough? But why mention it in a dying man's note unless it was to locate the centre of the trade.

He saw the distinctive coach leave; it picked up great speed as it manoeuvred onto the new road. Willoughby was about to follow it when something drifted across the road yards ahead and he realised what it was. The bonnet was unmistakable. It was Beth's. She must be in danger for he knew she would not have parted from her precious bonnet otherwise.

Beth had been left in a dark cellar with her hands tied behind her back; a rope from the tie had been thrown over a hook used normally for hanging pheasant. Her captors had taunted her before disappearing through a hatch.

Then she was alone, in the cold, damp, darkness.

After what seemed like ages the hatch reopened. She squinted, her arms aching as her legs weakened.

Then the unmistakable voice spoke to her.

"Beth, it's been quite a while, hasn't it, lass? Come over here and say hello to Oberon." The man's smile was as twisted as his wit. "Oh, no, you can't, can you, lass? The bird that flew the nest is all strung up, just waiting to be plucked."

Beth froze.

"Surely you've not had so many tups with Wilkes now that you've forgotten who you rightly belong to, eh?" He looked Beth up and down. "Still have a flat belly, though, that's good."

He rubbed his hand across her stomach. She felt her insides recoil. Spratt placed the lamp on a barrel. The life and joy that had animated her face only hours earlier had drifted away like the tide, to be replaced by an emotionless mask.

He raised his pistol. "Don't even want to give me a welcome smile? I bought you as a reward for Irwin Wilkes and, like a bad puppy, you bit the hand that fed you. I have a question that's been gnawing at me gut: Was that priest you ran with really worth losing your life for? Perhaps you can tell Oberon something he needs to know. Perhaps then I'll be nice to you." He traced her jaw line with his dirt-stained finger.

"Wouldn't hurt to untie me, would it? Me hands are almost dead and I think better when I'm not trussed up like a dead bird, Mr Spratt. The thing is, I knew there was something fishy about that priest and that's why I played along with him." Her mind was reeling; trying to invent any story that she could distract and fool the man with, knowing there was little if no chance of succeeding, but still desperate to try.

Spratt unhooked her hands. Her arms felt like two leaden limbs, detached from her body. He rubbed them roughly. Despite her revulsion at his touch she was relieved to feel blood move around them.

"How brave of you, and all the time we thought you'd just decided to run off. You see Wilkes's nose seems to have been reshaped by the priest. A holy mess, you might say. He is not a happy man." He took her skirt in his free hand, feeling the quality of her new dress. "Gone up in the world, lass, haven't you? Wilkes will be so pleased to hear of it." He flicked up the front of her hem with his hand.

Beth clenched her fists as she stood there motionless. She gently shook her head.

Spratt's hand reached under her skirts, grabbing Beth intimately. She flinched at his strength, sickened by his gesture, dreading what was to come.

"My you got stuff on underneath now, too. That's a novelty for our Beth, isn't it, lass? Smells sweeter too."

Beth said nothing, her skin, still so pale, gave no hint of embarrassment. He pointed his pistol at her face. It was as if her blood had turned to ice.

"Now, tell me what you are doing here. Fancy the sea air, did you?" He pulled his hand out from under her skirt and she let out a long low breath.

"No, it wasn't like that, Mister Spratt," Beth began to explain.

"What was it like, Beth? Travelling day and night with a preacher man must have been a new experience for you. You did leave with the preacher man, didn't you?" He started to unbutton her dress from the neck downwards. "Wilkes told me the reverend took a shine to you, right off. Stood up in the inn and preached about how he was to treat a lady. He was just too blind to see that there was none present."

"He was kind, Mister Spratt; he was a gentleman and treated me right." Beth looked anxiously at him. "He was nosy, though, and was trying to find out stuff about our way of life."

He stopped fiddling with her dress. "You unfasten this." He poked her chest with his finger tugging at the half open dress.

"Show me, Beth, what it was he saw in you." Spratt laughed. "I need reminding."

Slowly, she fumbled with the hooks and eyes. "He told me what I'd been doing was wrong and said I could have a life here that was different. Do an honest day's work, like, up at the big house. I was making me way there when I was jumped by your roughs," Beth continued slowly.

He grabbed Beth's arm. "Were you indeed? Fancied an honest job did you? Instead of a dishonest night's one!" He pulled her to him, kissing her roughly. She hated the taste and feel of him: tobacco, ale and sweat.

Spratt pointed towards the stairs, where a pile of empty coal sacks lay on the ground. He waved the pistol at her. "We need to celebrate our reunion, before we goes back to York. Think very carefully before you go disturbing Spratt's business!" He threw her down to the floor where the sacks were heaped. "Spread 'em out a bit. Make 'em right comfy." The pistol was placed on a large barrel at his side as he undid the buckle of his belt. "Take off your dress and let's see your finery. I ain't seen lace for quite some time; not on a young pretty wench, anyways." He slipped the leather belt from around his waist.

Beth slowly took off her gown and stood in the cold air, shivering. She had no wish for her new clothes to be spoilt.

"Keep going," he said, as he leaned against the stairs, blocking her only exit with the strap still in his hand.

Slowly, she slipped off the new cotton garments, exposing her full curves to his gaze. She bent down, noticing an old jug abandoned behind the bottom stair; she made her stretch deliberately low, knowing his eyes were fixed upon every movement of her body. She picked up her cherished clothes and folded them neatly, placing them on another barrel. He watched her in silence and she saw the pleasure in his devious grey eyes. But she had been looked upon by this man before and she kept telling herself she could cope with the humiliation just one last time — that's all it would be — just one last time and then she'd be free again. There was no going back to Wilkes for her. She had sampled freedom and she liked it. But first she had to face Spratt.

"You are a natural tease, girl. Born one and that is what you is good at. You please me now and I'll leave your beatings to Wilkes, when you return home. Come over here."

She forced herself to smile. As soon as she was within his reach he grabbed her by the throat and pushed her onto the sacks. His buttons scratched her skin as he fell atop her. She knew what he wanted to do next. He'd want to hurt her, she'd squeal, he'd bite, pinch and take her anyway he wanted and she was expected not to react, but be obedient and compliant. Beth swallowed, unseen by Spratt, she slipped her hand around the neck of the earthenware jug by the stair and held it tightly in her hand ready for that one moment of chance.

"Turn over," he ordered her.

As he eased his weight off her, she moved forward with his body as if to sit up.

"Wilkes should have fed you better. You look different somehow. You've been scrubbed too. Is that it? Does he like you clean, eh?"

With all the loathing she had for this man welling up inside her, she swung her arm around with one almighty force. The pot struck his skull hard with as much might as her hatred could spend. He collapsed onto the sacking and she hit him again, and again, not realising the jug had shattered. A jagged edge cut into his scalp. She stood up, shaking, looking at the blood dripping from the edge of the broken pot onto the grime of the sacks. Beth threw it down as if it had done the deed on its own and she could discard her guilt with it.

"I've killed him," she whispered as she stared at the blood seeping from him. "Think!" Willoughby will be waiting for me; she thought and repeated the words over and over again. She swallowed, he'd told her he wouldn't look for her if she wandered off, but he would, he had to ... she trusted him.

Beth wiped the blood from her hands on an unused sack and tried to quickly rub the dirt off her. She dressed as quickly as she could, remembering as she did that her bonnet, her lovely bonnet, had been lost. She threw the sacks over Spratt's body. In a confused state of indecision, she placed the tricorn on her head and wrapped his coat over hers. Beth made for the hatch, figuring if anyone saw her head appear, they would look the other way after seeing the hat, and not blow her brains out.

Willoughby dismounted, leaving the gig on the track. He couldn't risk taking it down to the inn. It would announce his presence, and as he entered at the front, if Beth had been taken in there, they could hide her or take her out of the back.

He ran over to the wall, tracing the path that Beth would have used. He followed the tracks and was surprised when a number of footprints seemed to be grouped around one particular area. He felt the stones with his bare hands, pushing them slightly until, sure enough, one gave way. He listened, putting his ear to a small gap, but heard nothing. He edged carefully inside; it seemed something had been stashed there. He quickly pulled back, replacing the loose stones. His attention returned to the ground where he could clearly see a set of footprints walking away. They were too big and too heavy to be Beth's but they led directly to the inn. The man was either huge, or carried a burden. Contraband? Beth?

"Hell and damnation!" he swore. There was only one way to find out if Beth was still there. He edged around to the back of the inn and found a cellar hatch. Willoughby primed his pistol and carefully made his way below the view of the small window towards the hatch door. As he reached the edge of it, it lifted up. He leaned flat against the wall, training his pistol on the opening door. A corner of a tricorn hat emerged. Spratt! He cursed to himself. Hoping the man was alone he leaned forward and grabbed him by the scruff of his wretched coat before he was seen.

Willoughby was surprised at how light he was. He slammed the man against the inn wall and kicked the hatch shut firm on anyone who may be following. With the pistol to Spratt's neck he quickly became aware that the figure he held wore a skirt, was too short, and was shaking in her boots — literally.

"Beth," he whispered.

"I killed him!" she whispered, her pitch high and her voice panicked.

"You killed Spratt?" Willoughby repeated.

"Aye, we got to get out of here."

Before either could think to say another word they were over the wall and making headway for the gig. Beth threw the hat down but Willoughby picked it up and rolled it quickly into Spratt's coat, before throwing them under their seat and setting off in the direction of the main road.

"Where now? London? The city might be good. Don't think they'd find us there." Beth started jabbering, spouting plans; New South Wales was mentioned, being missionaries so that she could try to make amends was another possibility.

Willoughby said nothing for some time until they had put miles between the inn and them. "You killed him, Beth. How?"

"He came at me. He wanted to have his pound of flesh. I played along until I could make a move and get out and then hit him hard with a pot, only it broke and I didn't see the sharp edge. It hit his head. Lots of blood see, on me; me clothes were folded up neat. Not on me clothes, just on me ... right dead, he was."

Her hand was shaking.

"Did he hurt you?"

"Not as much as he wanted to. Willoughby, they'll draw and quarter me if they finds me. I've got to get out of here."

Willoughby looked at her — small, frightened, and for once correct. He had to get her away, and fast.

# Chapter 17

"Willoughby, will you be wanted for stealing the gig if we don't go back?" Beth asked as she clung to his arm. She had not unwound herself from it since she had climbed aboard.

"Next to murder, what would that be to worry about? No, I left sufficient deposit for them not to search for it for a week at least. I had not intended to be hunted for a murder in my day clothes as well as in my uniform. I will have to dress as a fisherman soon." He smiled down at her, but Beth didn't respond.

"So you did expect to be hunted as a murdering priest?"

"No, I didn't. I will take you somewhere we can hide you, but Beth, as soon as we are able to, I shall have you sent far away to a place called Kent. No one will find you there. You will be safe on my estate and..."

"Your what?" Her head shot around as if she was seeing him anew. "Mr Willoughby, you really is a gentleman."

"You really are a gentleman, not 'is'." He smiled at her. "I shall arrange for a governess to teach you how to behave and speak correctly." He looked at her and stopped the gig. Tears had welled up in her sad eyes.

"You tease me. The only house I'll get is one of correction in the colonies and that's if I'm lucky. They want strong wenches out there so they'll spare me the rope and send me to the end of the world."

"I'm not teasing you. I'm serious, Beth. I took you on. I shall see you safe and you will have a life. First, we place you safely away. Then I need to do some work. You must stay where I put you, until I can arrange safe passage for you. You must trust me. I will join you, but it will be a little while. I have things to do here, which must not involve you. So dry your eyes, please, for now I need you to be strong."

"Yes, Mr Willoughby." She sniffed and breathed in the sea air as they made their way up the path over the headland of Stangcliffe, which was also the road to Ebton.

The old part of Ebton comprised of a group of fishermen's cottages nestled along the sandy bay, behind which the town was beginning to grow. The headland framed what had once been a village, sweeping down with sand dunes covered by wild marram grass. More modern terraced houses were being built on the higher land at the back of the town, and a wooded gill took the eye up towards the main coast road between York and Newcastle and to the moors beyond. It was wild, beautiful and as moody as the sea itself.

Willoughby saw the height of the cliff; he guessed it would be a three hundred feet drop. His chest tightened with grief as he realised that his beloved father had been thrown off it, either dead before or sent to a terrifying death. But by whom? How would he ever find out?

As they entered Ebton, they were looked upon with a wariness that made it obvious that visitors were still quite unusual despite the town's growth. They passed by a small inn. It looked as though it was built onto the beach itself. Crab pots and nets adorned the stretches of beach in between. This was a working town, but somewhere within it was Reverend Artemis Burdon. Beth looked as if she was filled with a renewed sense of panic. She clung to his arm. He drove onwards, taking the small road which led up towards the direction of a church spire.

They followed it up to the gates, passing by half the built houses along the way. The town was obviously growing in wealth. A new road was being laid to join them to the new improved network of coaching roads. Ebton's world, whether its local inhabitants liked strangers or not, was about to change and broaden.

They stopped in front of the lych gate and walked down the path towards the church. A grave digger was making his way around the side.

"Good morning," Willoughby said brightly. "Could you tell me where I might find the Reverend Artemis Burdon?"

The man placed his shovel, blade down, onto the grass and leaned on it. "Well, I could, but you won't thank me," he answered, and wrinkled up his face in what seemed to be a habitual gesture.

"Why would that be?" Willoughby asked, with a look of foreboding on his face.

"Well, he's over there, sir." The man pointed towards what was a recently dug grave with an elaborate headstone adorning it.

"What happened to him?" Willoughby asked.

"No, not the grave, sir, the vicarage beyond. He's in a foul temper, though," the man said dryly.

Willoughby glared at him and the man smiled back before shifting a little uneasily. "He had an accident. Went out riding and was found where his horse had thrown him."

Willoughby and Beth were shown into the vicarage by a rather severe looking lady wearing a dark grey dress, with a key chain at her side. She reminded Willoughby more of a gaoler than a housekeeper.

They were left in a dark crowded hallway. Plants, alongside riding boots and coats, greeted the unexpected guests. They stood close to each other as there was little room for them to do anything else.

The lady returned to them. "You may enter. I shall send Tristram around to fetch your vehicle and horse to the stables out back."

"Thank you, Miss…"

The lady looked around at Willoughby. "Mrs Hunter, sir."

"Sorry, Mrs Hunter. Thank you."

They were led through a low doorway to a room which had a big fire as its main focus. Two chairs were arranged either side of it. A rather plump man was seated in one with his foot up on a stool. He was sitting upon a large cushion.

"You'll excuse my not getting up, young Archibald, but the thing is I rather bruised my leg in an accident; most annoying and downright inconvenient." He nodded to his housekeeper who promptly left them, shutting the door behind her. "You must excuse her forthright manner. Neither her or her husband — you met him as you came across the church grounds — approve of me riding at my age. They think I'm past it." He smiled at Beth. "Now, Archibald, you are no longer your uncle's errant nephew. Plans must change. I have received word that a certain priest is being hunted."

"News travels fast in this part of the world, Reverend Burdon."

"Yes, in certain circles. I was expecting you, but you are to be my guest. You can no longer be employed here as my curate. Any new figure, whether genuine man of God or imposter will not be trusted now and word will quickly spread as you have already seen it can. You will not be righteous, pious or visible for long. You, sir, are in a deal of trouble. Who is this person? I can tell by her pretty face that she is well aware of your current problems."

For once Beth was silent. Willoughby looked to the older man. "She is as my sister, Miss Elizabeth; I need a place where

I can hide her until transport can be arranged for her to leave the area. I want to send her to our home in Kent, Rossington Hall. We need your help. Events have exploded before us and hampered my aims. I need to know Elizabeth will be safe then I can focus on other issues."

"There is only one man in the village I would trust her with but she will need to be silent and not wander." He looked from one to the other. "Beyond your unfortunate timing with the major, is there anything else I should know?"

Beth's eyes almost betrayed her fear. Willoughby answered, "Is that not enough?"

The man struggled to his feet, supporting his weight on a stick. "Stay here, young miss, you will now be known as Millicent, daughter of a family friend, if anyone asks. I shall have food brought to you. I and your young gentleman friend need to talk in my office. We won't be too long." He rubbed her cheek with his finger, but Beth shrank back into the chair.

"Why can't I be his sister, Elizabeth?"

"They are looking for a young wench called Beth. Is that sufficient reason?"

She nodded.

"Very good."

They walked across the narrow passage to a room opposite. Its only furniture was a cluttered desk, a makeshift shelving of books and a couple of chairs.

"Sit down, man." He made his way to one of the chairs and flopped uneasily into it as the leg gave way to his weight. "Who got to Husk?" he asked, as he tried to ease his position in the chair to a more comfortable one.

"Someone in the pay of a man called Oberon Spratt. He was subsequently disposed of in the Esk. If it was not for that young woman in there, I might have found myself invited to join him. Someone knew Husk had a list. Someone knew he had names, and one or all of them paid Spratt to silence him, but I arrived too late to save the major. Instead, my timely arrival would appear to have provided a screen that the murderers could escape behind."

The Reverend Artemis Burdon furrowed his brow. "How do you know he had a list unless he gave it to you before he died?"

"He spoke of it before he died, but they did not find it on him." Willoughby was loath to tell the whole truth, especially as Burdon's name was atop it.

"Did he tell you who was on it?"

"No, there was no time."

"First things first. We will have young 'Millicent' placed safely, and then you and I will have an honest and open exchange of information. I don't like strangers around my home, no matter how pretty they are, not unexpected ones. We have too much to do."

# Chapter 18

The reverend walked them down toward the village whilst leaning heavily on his walking stick.

Beth's eyes darted everywhere as she linked arms with Willoughby.

Burdon continued to chatter amiably to them, referring to his friends as Archibald and Millicent as they went past a couple of cottages and around the back of the inn on the edge of the beach. Nestling behind it was a building that looked like a small Wesleyan chapel, which he entered.

Beth's eyes widened as they fixed upon a black man, smartly dressed, who was stacking waxed tablets up on a table inside.

"Good morning, sir." His voice was both deep, well-spoken and confident. "Can I help you?"

"Yes," answered Reverend Burdon. "Abner, for once I believe you can."

"You need my help. I am honoured." He folded his arms casually across his waist-coated chest. Like the rest of his tall frame, the arms were muscular; apparently the man was strong in both character and build. Willoughby was surprised to see him in such a place, where the locals seemed to distrust anyone from outside their community.

"So you should be." The reverend waved Beth in. "I have a lost soul in need of a safe place to stay, somewhere quiet, until she can be whisked safely away to a more appropriate environment than we can offer her here. She is a stranger to these parts, which automatically makes her something to be wary of, as you well know.

"And what would you be wanting a safe place away from," Abner asked Beth.

"Someone who would enslave her," Willoughby said.

Abner looked at her, then glanced at him and nodded. "Well that's a good enough reason for me. Miss, will you trust me to look after you?"

Beth's eyes were wide as she stared at him, but she nodded.

Abner came nearer to her. "Have you been hurt, miss?"

Beth nodded again.

"Will you keep her hidden and safe until I can get her away from here?" Burdon asked.

"You know I will." He took hold of Beth's hand in his and gently rubbed the palm with his hand as if massaging it.

"Good, then we shall be about our business." The reverend gestured to Willoughby to leave.

Willoughby stepped forward towards Beth. "I will be back soon, Millicent."

She nodded, but still did not speak.

He looked at Abner. "Don't…"

Before he could finish Abner cut across Willoughby without letting go of her hand. "Don't even think of threatening me, man. I could crush you with my thumb." His words had even greater strength as he still gently rubbed Beth's small hand in his. "I'll help the young miss, because she is a broken spirit, and I mend broken spirits. Not because I've been threatened. You ask Abner — you don't tell him what to do or not."

Willoughby smiled. "I was about to say don't expect too much of her, she has had a traumatic journey, sir."

Abner laughed and nodded acknowledgement of Willoughby's words and at his presumptuous mistake.

The reverend returned to his office. Willoughby excused himself whilst he went to the gig to retrieve his coat, which he'd left over the seat covering Spratt's hat that he'd shoved in the space underneath. He wished now he had let it go to the wind, but instinct had told him to keep it.

He unstrapped his bag, placing it on the ground whilst he carefully concealed Spratt's coat within his greatcoat. He made sure no one saw him as he quickly felt around the inside of the hat. He found a hidden paper within the lining. Unfolding it he discovered it was a bond, drawn against a London bank, one he was familiar with. Then, satisfied that it held no other secrets he pushed it into the stove which was burning at the back of the stable block and closed it so that the flames finished it off. The bond was placed carefully within his wallet, and he waited a few moments until he was sure the hat would be burned. It was as he threw the coats over his arm that he felt something stiff hidden within the lining. In a pocket inside Spratt's was a despatch wallet. Here was not the time to examine it so he quickly dropped it into his bag and made his way back to the house. The stove was too small to take the man's coat.

Willoughby smiled at the housekeeper as he entered and was shown to a room. "The reverend is waiting for you in his office. I shall unpack your things for you, sir, whilst you talk with him." The housekeeper stepped back to let him leave.

"Please don't bother. I shall attend to my own things when I know how long I shall be here. Be as good as to tell Reverend Burdon that I will be down in a moment." He watched the disapproval cross the woman's face.

"As you like, sir." She left.

Willoughby closed the door. He hung his coat on the peg behind it and rummaged through Spratt's pockets. A small fire burned in the hearth so he tossed the useless items onto it. Money was placed to one side and left in a small table drawer. It could go to a donation to the chapel, he thought. No paper, no names, no times; an old pipe, tobacco and powder but nothing of any import. He bundled up the coat, emptied his clothes from his bag into the chest of drawers and shoved Spratt's coat within it, leaving only the despatch wallet on the bed.

He quickly opened it. The information was copied from government documents: maps and plans of defences of the realm. Spratt was passing on information. Was Napoleon planning to invade Britain? His navy had been gathering force and appeared prepared. Spratt must be the key person that Nathaniel sought, and Beth had snuffed him out. Now they had a dead end and, with his death, the next piece of the puzzle was lost. He placed the papers within his jacket pocket and made his way down to the reverend's study.

# Chapter 19

Burdon came straight to the point. "Willoughby, what secrets do you hold from me? Whatever you kept from that lass, you need to tell me. If Major Husk has been murdered then I am also in danger and you, sir, may have brought the harbinger of evil to my very door." He rested both hands on the desk in front of him.

"What can you tell me about Mrs Ingham, my father and the alum mine owned by her husband and a financier in London?" Willoughby asked.

"Very well, if I must show trust in you first, then so be it." The man wiped his balding head with his kerchief, watching Willoughby as he began to explain. "Joshua was in love with the lady — and I use the term very loosely as befits her morals. She caught him by the ... heart strings. His normal good sense was lost, and with it his life. She has expensive tastes, hates this area and will do anything and go anywhere to be within society. Her husband gives her free rein to do as she wishes so long as she is there when he requires her and her indiscretions are kept discreet. Your father was like a puppy in her presence, full of life and play. A good man, but she won his trust. Joshua was fool enough to believe her." He sighed and shook his head. "He even shared his mission with her, asking for help to become closer to the people her husband mixed with. He made a very simple mistake. He suspected the man, but not the lady."

Willoughby felt slightly uneasy. He had not fallen in love with Beth, but he was trusting her as she was him. Different circumstances but, with his previous indiscretion with

Charlotte, he had already had one clear warning from Nathaniel. Now he knew why his uncle had shadowed him. He had already seen Willoughby's father fall because of his heart ruling his head.

"You mean she is behind the selling of intelligence?" Willoughby asked.

"No, she could not have enough knowledge of affairs of state for that. She is not the leader but one of his puppets. Her husband may be in it for the money and the contraband, but I had no notion that he was a traitor. He turns a keen profit. His partner…"

"Simon!" Willoughby suggested, thinking of his father's note.

Burdon looked surprised. "I do not have any knowledge of a Simon. His partner, who has never been seen in the region, is known only as Mr King. He provides the routes via his shipping concerns. I do not know Ingham well. He is a serious sort of chap, who keeps his own council. Him I would watch. The alum industry has ships legitimately sailing to London and Newcastle on a regular basis. They employ the locals who are low paid and work intermittently, but who need to provide their own revenue from smuggling."

"You condone the trade?"

Burdon was taken aback. "Not condone, but understand their needs and minds; it is self-interest. But I will never understand a man who sells the land from under his countryman's feet. Napoleon is our enemy. He has been building a fleet and we suspect may be planning to invade. The money from contraband fills his coffers; this the locals do not understand. These people need money, so they turn a quick coin and do not choose to look at a deeper picture. However, they are on the whole not deliberate or willing traitors.

Someone who understands the situation fully, most certainly is."

"Ingham's name was on the list that Husk had written," Willoughby confessed.

"Then you do have the list? I suspected as much. Lose it," he replied, his face serious. "It will bring nothing but death to your door. Know the names but burn the list."

"I saw it. It was not long. If they think I still have it they will hunt me anyway."

"Who else was named?" The reverend looked at him intensely.

"Spratt, one Mr Ingham and yourself." Willoughby stared back at him, remembering the note. "Tell me, sir, about Mrs Ingham. Did she love Father?"

"'Mother Ingham' they call her, behind her back, after the mother liquid at the alum mine. It takes out all the badness from the alum. That's what she is — pure, selfish badness. The irony is she is childless."

"Did she have a hand in my father's murder?" Willoughby asked.

"As far as I know she did not directly have Joshua killed. I believe she was affected by his death because for a time she was not seen afterwards. It may have been fear, caution or as near to love as she is capable of, but she did not socialise for a time, as if in mourning." He looked at Willoughby thoughtfully. "Tell me, is it your mission to unearth a murderer or stop a traitor, sir?"

"Both. I believe one will lead to another."

"Then you had better seek out a man called Oberon Spratt. He wears a tricorn hat, skulks around inns and it is my belief it was he who killed Joshua. You will have to be quick because he... What is wrong?" Burdon stared at Willoughby whose fists had clenched into balls at his side as he stood up.

"Spratt murdered my father?" Willoughby felt the muscle in his abdomen tighten. He had crossed paths with the man he sought, even exchanged words with him, not knowing he was the murderer. No wonder Spratt had thought him familiar. Now his body lay in a cellar, killed by a terrified wench. Willoughby did not feel relieved but in some way cheated of the justice he craved.

"I believe so, but he is a difficult man to find and I have no proof that would hold up in a court of law. He works directly with his backer. Locals know who is in the trade along their own coast or village, but he is the man who finds the money and knows the contacts, who organises the runs, stashes and then sells goods to the Frenchies. Find and follow him and you will eventually locate your man. Let him find you first and you are a dead man, sir."

"Then we have lost the trail and all hope, unless Mrs Ingham can help."

"How so?" Burdon asked, not understanding.

"Spratt is already dead, sir."

"What! Without him everything will fall apart. The trade will lie in ruins." Burdon stood, and limped back and forth a few paces, a grim expression upon his face. "Gangs will spring up and a new link man will rule once the battle for chief place has been established. The source of Spratt's betrayals will go to ground as soon as he learns of Spratt's demise. This could set us back years and with Napoleon possibly preparing for an invasion. Does your uncle know of Spratt's demise?"

"No, I have not yet notified him."

"Spratt may have been essential to the smooth working of the ring but, more importantly, he is the man who is expected to pass the secrets on to his French counterpart in two days' time. Where, and to whom I do not know, but the date I do, for I too have my spies, and a very good one has told me this."

Willoughby produced the documents he had taken from Spratt's coat and flung them on the desk. "He won't be trading them this week, Reverend, but I need to know from whom they came and the only man I know who could tell me this is my uncle. I shall have to return to York before laying my accusations before Ingham, and you, sir, I must entrust with the safety and well-being of young Beth."

"Very well. I can assure you that Abner will keep her safe. Willoughby, agents cannot carry baggage. You must let her go. Your only goal has to be to find this man."

# Chapter 20

Beth stared at the man seated across the small table from her. She looked at his face, hardened by life, yet his eyes were not. Beth wondered what they had witnessed; more horror than her own, she suspected. She felt he was a kindred spirit — they had both been through pain and survived.

"So, Miss Millicent, how did you come to be travelling with a Rossington?"

Beth looked at Abner wide-eyed, surprised by the question. "A what?"

"I knew who he was the moment he entered the chapel. It was me who found his father's body washed ashore four or five years since. That man is the image of his father before him. Coincidence then that he should be here, isn't it?"

"He calls himself Mr Willoughby, he saved me from people who hurt me and that's all I know of him," Beth said defensively.

"Where did he find you?" Abner leant casually back in his chair, crossing his arms across his broad chest.

"In an inn." Beth tilted her chin up, looking into his eyes.

"Well, Miss Millicent, fill your lungs with the fresh air of the sea, for you are free from it now. You shall not have to suffer taunts, breathe in smoke-filled tallowed air or work your way for your next meal. Can you tell me why you need to be spirited away? If you don't confide in me I could place you in more danger than you are in at the present time, without meaning to."

"I killed a man." Beth's hand started to shake again as she cupped it in her lap. She stared at it blankly. She sobbed, just thinking about the fate that would befall her if she was found.

Abner leaned forward. He reached down and held her hands in his, calming them until her trembling ceased. She felt his warmth as he gently rubbed them with coarse and calloused skin of his own. When they stilled, he spoke. "Why and who, miss, did you kill?"

"He attacked me. He was going to take me back to the inn and they would have killed me — slowly. I'm nothing to them. I meant to knock him out. I didn't know it would kill him ... I ... I killed him, Abner. God help me, I killed Spratt!" She stared at Abner's face as a wave of shock crossed it. "Please don't hand me to them. Please..."

"Oh, little one. What trouble Burdon has brought to my door this day." He stood up and led her by the hand up a narrow flight of steps to the upstairs room. Here a large, roughly made four poster bed had pride of place under the open thatch of the cottage's roof. Beth tried to pull her hand away from his. She feared that she had spoken in haste. Her trust had been wrong. She wanted Willoughby. She needed Willoughby ... she was scared.

"Millicent, calm yourself. Be still now!" Abner pulled her in front of him so that she was spun gently into the room. He stayed blocking the doorway but did not enter. "Listen, please, stay here ... on your own, and sleep. I'll not touch you and no one else will enter this place. My word upon it — on the Bible if you wish. I will lock the door and you shall have your own space in which to rest; do not light the lamps when the sky darkens. I won't betray you, but it is just as well for you to trust me, because I will now have to choose your escape route with great care. You will not be ferried away by the local fishermen for they all know Spratt well and fear him and his men. Sleep well, miss. You are safe here."

Beth was confused and tired, and she pined for the man who had only recently figured so importantly in her life. She wanted her Mr Willoughby back. She crawled into the big bed and covered herself with the blankets. They had Abner's musk on them. She wrapped herself in them desperately wanting to feel protected again. What he was she did not know, but she looked at her hand, it had stopped trembling; she remembered his touch and with a sense of calm he had given her she slipped into a much needed slumber.

Beth slept soundly and awoke some hours later. Looking to the chair in her room she was surprised to see a woman sitting in it.

"Lord!" She sat up.

The woman chuckled at her outburst.

It was no spectre but a real person, perhaps six summers older than Beth was, but very neat. The interior of the room belonged to a far grander home than the humble cottage. She was filled with such a peculiar feeling as she looked at the lady sitting upright, reading a book, in the chair next to her bed. It was, she realised, an overwhelming sensation of fear. Where was she? Who was the stranger? Beth had met too many strangers recently, her world had changed so much and she had travelled so far. She did not care to meet yet more.

"Do you feel better now?" the woman asked gently.

"Yes, I'm sorry for ... I must tell Mr Will ... Reverend Archibald ... that I am well." Beth swung her legs out from between the two crisp linen sheets.

"You can't tell him anything, my dear. He has had pressing business that needed attending to most urgently. Do you remember being left with Abner? You have slept a while because he gave you a mild draught. Your friend asked us to give you his deepest and sincerest apologies and to convey a promise that he would return to you as soon as he could, and to remind you that he gave you his word you would be safe." She patted Beth's hand. "And I don't think you need worry. I am sure he will return to you as soon as he is able to." Her smile was warm and reassuring.

"But we have not known each other very long and such bad things have happened in what is a very short time. He may be in a good deal of danger. He needs me to look out for him, but he might think that I'm jinxed..." Beth said. "He shouldn't have ridden off on his own. He needs me, he is too good for them ... he won't see the danger."

"I doubt that, but I know, miss, that you have been troubled by circumstances, which is why I have suggested Abner watches over your friend."

"Abner?"

"You are safe here, Miss Millicent."

"Who are you?" Beth asked.

"I teach here. I own this house and Abner is my dearest friend. I owe him my life and my happiness. He is a very special person to me, Miss Millicent. I hope you can accept him, as I do. You were not safe in the village; he had to get you away quickly. You are being hunted by some very bad men."

The door to the room opened and Abner appeared wearing a greatcoat and wide-brimmed hat. He held a rifle in his right hand.

"You awoke earlier than I thought you would, Millicent. Do not fear, but stay here. Miss Tully will see you are looked after well and keep you out of sight. I am now going to find your Mr Willoughby. I think he may be in greater danger than he estimates."

"What am I expected to do then, just wait here?" Beth asked.

"It's what women are supposed to do, isn't it?" Miss Tully answered pointedly, but with an impish glint in her eye.

Beth watched her. She was graceful, but there was an inner strength about her that Beth sensed and admired. She wondered if she had been like Miss Tully, would Willoughby have viewed her differently.

Willoughby had grabbed a few hours of much needed sleep, and before dawn, gratefully accepted the use of Burdon's fine horse and rode as fast as it would take him to the Old Flagon Inn on the York road. One man could give him the information he desperately needed to know and no doubt the proof that was essential to break the ring. It was time to find him.

Willoughby was troubled. The despatches had held news of the Admiralty's intentions to foil Napoleon's plans. As he thundered along the road, he repeated the words to himself, Mother I ... a reference with a double meaning; she carried an impure load — messages for the French and the 'In '... standing for Ingham — his father's mistress. He grimaced. Who was Simon? He must be the man. How naïve he had been. Like father like son. Willoughby chided himself as his anger drove him relentlessly onwards.

# Chapter 21

Willoughby approached the inn where he had first seen Spratt. Willoughby was sure that this was where he had picked up the papers from the Jezebel, Ingham. He dismounted and tied the horse's reins to a stable door behind the inn. He crossed the yard; the fresh air outside was a stark contrast to the smoky atmosphere and dusky tallow lit lamps within the Flagon Inn. As he stepped over the threshold, Willoughby saw two men drinking by the open hearth; it crackled and spluttered as the fire burnt. The other tables were empty. He approached the innkeeper, who from behind his serving counter did not speak or acknowledge his presence. Willoughby could see the empty chair where Spratt had been seated by the bay window. The innkeeper knew the answers and Willoughby was determined to find them out. Willoughby needed evidence and if it meant dragging the man back to Nathaniel, then drag him he would.

The innkeeper finally looked his way. "Drink?" he asked, and Willoughby noted that he had a scar across his cheek, which partially explained his permanently sombre appearance.

"I'm looking for a man, and I think you might be able to help me find him." Willoughby saw the innkeeper's eyebrows rise. "His name is Mr Oberon Spratt. He wears a tricorn hat and drinks here."

"If I did know who you're talking about, who would I say is asking for him?" Willoughby noticed the man's eyes were looking beyond him, glancing over his shoulder in the direction of the men sitting by the fire.

"If you know where he's hiding, tell him that the priest wants to talk with him," Willoughby answered, and slipped his hand into his greatcoat pocket finding his small pistol. "It will be worth his while to find me," Willoughby added.

Spratt was missing, no shadow of suspicion must fall upon him, but in order to pick up the trail, to be certain, he must make the man talk. Intent on this task, he momentarily ignored the presence of the other customers. Willoughby's arms were grabbed. His hand was slammed down on the counter, sending the pistol scuttling across the floor.

"What do you know about Spratt?" the innkeeper asked, as he picked the weapon up, turning it over in his hand.

Willoughby tried to pull away from their vice-like grip. Overpowered, he stood no chance. In his desperation he realised he had made the wrong move. "Not a lot, which is why I am trying to find him. I want to make a deal — put business his way." Willoughby saw the innkeeper considering his words.

"What kind of business?" the man asked, pointing the pistol directly at his eyeball.

Willoughby spoke his words carefully. "That would be between us. He does his own deals. Spratt does not rely on others."

"When did you last see him?" the innkeeper asked, which confirmed Willoughby's fears; these men were anxious. They did not know where Spratt was; which meant that word had not reached them yet of his death.

"In here," Willoughby replied, and winced as they tightened their grip on his arms, pushing them painfully up his back, "on my last journey through here, which is why I have returned. You served me then, remember? I spoke to Spratt outside the inn before the soldiers arrived. They arrested me, but I escaped."

The man knocked Willoughby's hat to the floor. He looked at his two friends. "It's the man they're looking for! He poisoned the major! Who the hell are you and what's your game?" he shouted into Willoughby's face.

"I've told you, I've business with Spratt, for his ears only, not his lackeys! If there is trouble, I can help. You know the soldiers are after me," Willoughby said firmly as the pistol barrel touched the skin by his temple.

The sound of a rider outside interrupted their conversation.

"Take him around the back, lads, and find out what he's playing at. See if he knows what's happening with Spratt. He never missed a drop before." The innkeeper clipped Willoughby hard across the back of his head before he was dragged off.

He was half-dragged outside to the end stall of the stables. They threw him down on the soiled hay and cracked their knuckles as they formed fists. Luckily, Willoughby's hand closed around the staff of a half-buried hay fork. He grabbed it, holding the points towards them. His decision was met with scorn, but at least it gave him a fighting chance, even if it was a very small one. The first man stepped towards him; Willoughby jabbed the fork toward his belly. Instantly his friend grabbed it from the side, whilst the first man planted a fist in Willoughby's gut. Doubled up as a pain shot through his body, the wind knocked from him, Willoughby fell to his knees cursing.

Beth's face flashed through his mind. She been brought low how many times, but never had her spirit broken. He had a burning desire to survive like never before. In the past, he had been driven by the memory of his father, to serve and obey for the honour of a dead man's memory and name. Now he knew he wanted to live not only to respect his father's memory, but live his own life and love who he willed. He pictured the young, spirited runaway and realised how much she desired that also. He straightened up to his full height and ran at the nearest man, driving his shoulder hard into the man's belly, but ricocheted off him as if he was a child. Another hit sent him flying to the back wall of the stall, followed by the loud guffaws of his abusers.

"Now talk, whilst you still can," one of them said, as he reached up to a hook on the wall and removed a driver's whip.

"I'm looking for the man, Spratt," Willoughby answered, gasping, trying to keep calm and bluff his way out of the hapless situation he had stupidly walked into. He wiped away a trickle of blood from the corner of his mouth.

"Ain't we all? Now, where was the last time you saw 'im?" The man toyed with the drivers' whip. "I ain't never taken the skin off a pretty white boy before, Jake," he said to his friend. "First time for everything, eh?"

"Always a first time, Seb," the other answered, and Willoughby, despite his determination to hide his fear, swallowed hard.

He clenched his fists ready for one more attack, but they stood like a solid wall in front of him.

"Shame to spoil your fun, gents, but his skin is staying exactly where it is." Abner's voice surprised Willoughby as much as it did the other two men. They turned around to fight him, but found themselves facing a rifle, primed and aimed directly at one of their stomachs. Willoughby quickly got to his feet and edged around them, until he was standing next to Abner.

"So glad to see you," he said.

"Couldn't have you roaming around the moors and getting lost, could I?" Abner answered, but his eyes were fixed on the men.

Willoughby held the weapon whilst Abner tied them up.

"Now, let me ask you the same question. Why does Spratt come here? How do you contact him? Who does he meet and why?" Willoughby asked, and gave Abner the gun back, whilst he picked up the whip and cracked it just in front of them as they had done to him. They both flinched, one more than the other, so Willoughby directed all his questions to the weaker man.

"Don't know. He was supposed to make a meeting at the Cruck Inn yesterday and a drop 'ere, but he didn't show at either. No one's seen him, it's like he's vanished." The man was visibly trembling and the other was cursing his frightened friend's cowardice. "There's a big landing that's been missed. He better have a good excuse or 'e'll be in big trouble. The money doesn't like their investments goin' astray. They'll be out for 'is blood." The man's spittle dripped down his front as he continued to shake.

Willoughby was disgusted at how soon the man had turned into a snivelling wreck.

"Gag them. We need to talk to the innkeeper." Willoughby brushed himself down. His stomach and jaw ached, but he stood proud and walked back into the inn.

Without looking up, the barman asked, "Did he speak, then?"

"Yes, but then I often do in polite society," Willoughby replied, and the man reached for the pistol from under the counter. But it was Abner whose words stopped him mid action. "I wouldn't do that, Zach."

"Abner, what you doin' here and with the likes of him?" Zach put both hands on the counter.

"He needs a little bit of information, that's all. He's no threat to you."

"Spratt seems to have disappeared and many are asking where and why. He let the drop go and there's a growing panic about the place. No one knows if he's a turncoat or if summat's happened to him. Then this piece of quality walks in as bold as brass and wants to chat with him. I told the boys to play with him a while and see if we could find out what's happenin'. But I didn't know he was with you. You best take him away before the boys get upset again." The innkeeper attempted a smile at Willoughby.

Abner nodded. "Willoughby, we best leave. There is nothing here for you to learn."

Willoughby picked up his hat from the floor and brushed it with his fingers. "Tell me who he was last seen with … please?" he asked, and watched Zach as he looked to Abner before replying. The man slid the small pistol across the counter towards Willoughby, who put it back into his pocket.

"He was at Whitby, made a collection. He was supposed to meet the man here, in the back room as always, but he didn't come. The man don't wait around. Never speaks and no one knows where he comes from. No one has seen him since he finished his business there. He could have heard summat bad was goin' down and taken to a boat to London or to some other heathen place. Spratt may have high-tailed it back to his homeland in Kent, perhaps. Always said he'd return and live like a gent in a big house down there one day." He glanced at Abner. "No offence meant about heathens." Abner's expression did not change so Zach continued. "He could even be with the Frenchies by now. Who knows what that man would do if he was up against it?"

"The man that comes, could it be Jacob or Wilkes from York?"

"Neither, Wilkes stays put, Jacob only comes before a run. No, he meets a cloaked gentleman's man, with a high hat and a dark scarf, out back. He don't give names. Don't want to be seen and slips off like the devil himself."

"Who is Simon?" Willoughby asked.

"No one that I knows of." The man shrugged.

Willoughby and Abner left the inn, riding out onto the moor road. Abner kept his gun handy, eyes ever vigilant.

"Where is Beth?" Willoughby was battered, bruised and frustrated.

"Safe. I left her in the town — away from the village. When I return I will take her to Whitby in a boat, then I suggest you both return to London or wherever you're from. Stay well away from here."

"How important to the ring is Oberon?" Willoughby asked.

"Very. He was the link joining two halves of a very profitable chain." Abner stared out over the moor, as if listening for any sound that didn't belong.

"You said 'was'."

"Aye, she has done us all a great service. The man who killed your father is dead. The ring will fall. You should be glad. The authorities will pick up the remnants and them that survive will continue with the trade that is left and eventually thrive."

"Spratt definitely killed my father?"

Willoughby did not feel satisfied. He had wanted to face his father's murderer and arrest him personally; to see justice done, not to murder the man himself, because then he would be no better than him. Certainly he had never dreamed a young woman would do the job for him, to be scarred for the rest of her life at the memory whilst all the other blackguards disappeared like grains of sand onto a beach. The person who betrayed his country and own kind would answer to him, though. 'Good' was not the word to describe how he felt, for the bitterness was almost tangible.

"Which link are you, Abner, and does the Reverend Burdon know that you consort with rogues?" Willoughby watched as the man just laughed. He wondered if Burdon should have been trusted after all. Had he hood-winked him? If so, how safe would Beth be?

"Burdon knows as much as he chooses to. He is careful not to make judgements. Which link am I? Possibly your missing one, Willoughby," he answered, and kicked his horse onwards. Willoughby followed him as they headed back to York.

# Chapter 22

Willoughby did not ease his pace until he saw the gothic towers of the great cathedral in the distance.

"Where are we going?" Abner asked, as he rode up alongside Willoughby.

"I have to report my findings. It is better that you do not accompany me."

"You look rough." Abner ignored his other comment.

"I will freshen up once I have seen him, for this cannot wait. For once, my business must come first. I must stop the rot before I can return to Beth and to Whitby. From there we will take passage direct to London."

"Beth was born to the gutter. Do you think you are being kind to her to raise her up from her squalor only to be looked down upon by your kind? They would sniff her out, she'd never be accepted within 'society'."

"She should have a basic education at least. Beth is not lacking in intelligence, just opportunity of finding someone who would care for her." He steadied his horse as it flicked its mane.

"What about Spratt?"

"I thought I needed the 'Spratt' to catch the mackerel," Willoughby answered. "Now, I shall have to try and catch this particular fish without any bait. Perhaps you should wait out here where you will be safe until I return." Willoughby looked at the large man who had travelled alongside him, and saw his grin broaden.

"Listen, white man, I learned to look out for myself many years ago. I'm a free man and it is you who are in more danger than I, believe me." Abner patted Willoughby's back. The strength of the friendly gesture hurt as he slapped him on a recently acquired bruise.

If his fist delivered a punch with that force, Willoughby thought, it would knock a man senseless. Better to have him as a friend at your back than an enemy facing you.

"Abner, what part in this ring do you play? Why do they accept you and let you move freely amongst them?" Willoughby watched his dark eyes; even in the half light they were clear and proud.

Abner held his gaze. "Which ring do you refer to? The one that supplies over-taxed goods at a discount to 'honest' traders, or the one that trades a country's secrets? I have learnt to love this land and its strange ways, despite all its faults. Why would I betray it to our enemies? How would I have the means? It could be said that I have reason enough, but I am not the sort that turns on their place of living."

"Neither is right, Abner. Both break the law, both kill." Willoughby saw his derisory look.

"War kills. The slavers kill. Poverty kills. Magistrates hang starving children for stealing bread. Tell me, sir, when is it not murder to kill and when is it 'just'?" He looked away from Willoughby whilst waiting for his response.

"Do you preach? You have the gift of putting over your point very clearly." Willoughby watched the man take pride in his comment.

"Only to children; the adults prefer to listen to Artemis Burdon; ask him where his brandy, baccy and cloth comes from."

"So why do they accept, Abner?"

"Your father was not the only one to be washed up on that shore. I was on a ship that was wrecked. I saved myself and four others. One of them was Amos from the inn. If he accepts you, then everyone will."

"Ride with me then, and let's end the second ring." Willoughby patted Abner's back with what he hoped was equal and impressive force, which resulted in his new friend chuckling. Willoughby wondered how deeply Abner was mixed up in the trade, and more so how he would keep the man out of harm's way should the authorities follow through with removing them all. Was he one of the loose ends that would be caught?

"Very well, but I tell you, if you find out who Ingham's partner is, then you'll find out who the money is behind Spratt's ring."

Willoughby nodded. He already had a suspicion, but he still needed to prove that his theory was true.

Willoughby and Abner entered the city and stabled the horses safely, then calmly started walking back towards the row of new terraced houses.

Abner, with his gun held under his great caped coat, stayed at the corner of the road in the shadow of a large oak tree. Willoughby nodded, continuing to approach the familiar house. He paused, breathed deeply, knowing full well that he looked a mess again. This time not soaking wet, but covered in mud from his scuffle with the two men at the inn. He had wiped the blood from the corner of his mouth and hoped he could still look as if he was in control of the situation. He raised the knocker and let it drop to make a loud clatter.

Crombie half opened the door, and let him enter without exchanging a word, but cast a cursory glance down Willoughby's soiled coat.

The servant announced him to his uncle, who had not yet retired. He was led down the same corridor to the room at the end of the hall. Willoughby thought he saw a movement in a doorway to his left; he caught his aunt's lavender perfume as he passed by the open door. His aunt did not step out to welcome him. She had more discretion or sense, he thought.

It was with a heavy heart that he entered his uncle's office because he knew this time he had failed in his mission. He had information; he had some answers, but also many questions left unanswered and his theory lacked the tangible proof he needed. Beth had removed the man who would have brought the whole cancerous ring crumbling down.

Nathaniel was sitting behind his large mahogany desk, his hands resting fingertip to fingertip in front of him, as he leaned on his elbows and watched Willoughby's dishevelled appearance as he approached. Willoughby noticed he too had tired eyes.

"I was not expecting you to return so soon, Willoughby. Do you have a name for me?" Nathaniel sat back in his chair and folded his arms across his buttoned up black jacket. The tense grip he had on his arms showed in his hands.

"I have more than one name, sir. Major Husk passed a list to me before he was poisoned." Willoughby stood before him and waited for his superior's response.

"I understand you are wanted in connection with his murder, and that of a soldier, too. You have managed to have half the dragoons of Yorkshire looking for your priestly persona. I congratulate you on at least escaping with your life, even if you appear to have left your wits behind you in Whitby. You are failing in more ways than one — or should I say flailing! I suppose that is why you have come skulking back here. Bad show, Willoughby. In that state the militia or dragoons will most likely sniff your trail to my very door! Could you not have gone to Reverend Burdon as I ordered you to and lay low as his curate?" He sighed deeply. "Do you have the list with you?" Nathaniel held out his hand and Willoughby placed the piece of paper in it.

"Ingham. Well, he is no longer a suspect." Nathaniel took his quill and crossed the name off.

"Why, sir?"

"I know him."

"You told me to trust no one, sir." Willoughby was staring at the man opposite, his own words resounding in his head. "Is he a business acquaintance of yours, Uncle?"

Nathaniel did not answer his question. "If he is somehow involved in the smuggling ring, do you have any proof? He will be arrested as soon as we have that. If he is guilty you must provide evidence. Mrs Simone Ingham is a respected figure within the area." His uncle stared at him sombrely. "Do you have the proof of her husband's involvement in either the smuggling activities of contraband or intelligence?"

"Simon!" Willoughby muttered, then said aloud to his uncle: "No ... I have no direct proof, but I suspect that goods are smuggled in the ships used for transporting the barrels of urine from London to the north." Willoughby stared back into his uncle's eyes. "Her husband will be aware of this as he and his partner have worked the scheme successfully together for years. Both will have benefitted richly from it."

"I'll have the ships intercepted." Nathaniel looked back at the list. "Oberon Spratt?" Nathaniel raised both eyebrows at the name.

"A mysterious illusive figure who was known for wearing a tricorn hat, I believe."

"And you could not locate him." Nathaniel stood up and leaned over the desk towards Willoughby. "Is this all you have to offer?" A patch of high colour heightened his cheeks. Then he paused. "You said 'was', what do you mean?"

"Yes, sir, for he is now dead."

Nathaniel's colour changed as his blood drained from his cheeks.

It was then Willoughby knew that he stared at the face of a traitor; not only to the country but to the whole of the Rossington family. Ingham was not his man. Nathaniel had been so close to him he could never have seen the truth. Willoughby was so like his father in looks and nature, but his upright uncle had taken his sharp features and the character of his mother's family and cold nature. So loved and trusted by his brothers that they could never have seen him for the evil he represented.

"Why report back to me with such unsubstantiated claims to the guilty when a man as honourable as Major Husk lies dead? Willoughby, your father will be turning in his grave at your futile efforts." Nathaniel adopted his usual stance, standing by the mantelpiece with his hands behind his back. "You have killed the one man who could have drawn all parts of the ring together. You are a fool — a total imbecile! You should have watched him, not killed him!"

"I agree with you, Uncle, Father would be outraged, but not at my botched efforts, but at the truth behind the identity of the traitor who placed his own nephew in the line of fire, hoping he would no doubt join his father." Willoughby watched the impassive eyes of his uncle. What he had always seen as the stern determination of a patriot, a duty bound man devoted to his country, he now saw as a man with no honour, but the desire to own the whole of the Rossington fortune, plus whatever the French were paying him to commit treason. How else did he know Spratt was the key to unlock the truth? "Did you own Simone, as you did Francesca?"

Nathaniel's lips curled slowly into a smile. "So, my little priest has a theory, unsubstantiated and unproven. I must congratulate you; you failed both as an agent and as a 'man of God' or should I say 'boy'? Do you realise you are wanted for the murder of two men? I only have to send for my manservant and you would be thrown in gaol for the duration. You would certainly not survive to come before the magistrate, that would be assured. Willoughby, how you have disappointed me! You could not even go to your own grave with success. Will you call me out or try to run me down here?"

"'*Mother* I', I realised that it referred to the woman Ingham, a dangerous beauty and no doubt my father's mistress. She looked as though she had seen a ghost when she faced me. I wondered if, as you inferred, the head of all evil was in fact a woman, but no. You had an agent like her working for you in York. You manipulate her kind for your own will. Tell me, did you place her in Father's path?" Willoughby asked.

"Temptation, Willoughby, a strong enemy of mankind. He enjoyed it whilst it lasted." Nathaniel stared boldly at him, showing no remorse for his actions.

"These women play a dangerous game, but it is you who holds the winning cards. When Major Husk's murder happened in front of my own eyes, it occurred to me that you were the only constant link to these people: my own uncle, who sent out my father before me. Tell me, did you kill one or two of your own brothers?" Willoughby's hand rested in his pocket, his pistol ready within his fingers.

Nathaniel stood unmoved by his words. "So now you have your theory, what do you expect to do with it? Shoot me in my own study? Do you think you would escape from such a blatant murder charge? And what would become of your dear aunt if you did? No, Willoughby, you can take your theory to your grave with you, for I am too powerful for you to bring down. You are soft; you could do nothing to hurt your Aunt Eliza. She would be destroyed the moment you killed me. And lest we forget, to kill breaks a commandment, Willoughby. You are an outlaw; no one will listen to the failed priest who sinned unforgivably. You are as vermin; Satan's scum, they would shout at your hanging. Sad, one brother has died a hero's death fighting for King and country in a foreign land and the other will perish as a traitor to that same king, a murderer and an abomination before God!"

Willoughby stood stock still. "Charles is dead?"

"Yes. He fell behind enemy lines. Whilst you have been failing so miserably at your own task, I granted him his wish to sell his commission and return to our shores if he stood in one more battle to try and distinguish himself. He was in the front line, leading his men to victory. He received special orders to take command. Charles just wasn't cut out to be a soldier, but his name will live on to honour the family." Nathaniel's smile was too much for Willoughby. He launched himself at him but his uncle moved swiftly, still taking some of the force of Willoughby's fist to his gut. He spun around and drew a rapier from its mount on the wall behind him and lunged at Willoughby. Moving back, the sharp blade cut through Willoughby's greatcoat and drew a trickle of blood from his arm. He rolled backward over the desk, but Nathaniel trained a pistol at him.

"You will leave this office, Willoughby. Do not fret, now. I will not kill you here. Too messy. Too many questions and too distressing for Eliza; she would give me hell." He smiled. "You will run and then you shall be chased across this sorry land. Shortly, you will be imprisoned. However, take solace in the knowledge that you will not be the son who is seen as a disgrace to this family. No one knows the true identity of the bungling Reverend James. He will hang at dawn, alone and unobserved, and Mr Willoughby James Rossington will be reported to have died on board a ship bound for the colonies, a man seeking his fortune, but alas taken too soon. Someone who never even had the opportunity to set foot on heathen land. A travesty — destiny or God's will. You can call it what you will. So some element of truth will linger. Your aunt will grieve for you as she has your father," he said and smirked. "You see, dear Willoughby, the barren woman who could not sire me an heir, married the wrong brother, but your father was too weak to contest my match. The real love of his life was his beloved Eliza, but he could only look on her at a distance, because he was a man of honour. I strongly suspect she would have happily warmed his bed, but he had too much respect for her and his brother's position. 'Love' and 'compassion' are the two weakest words created by mankind. So instead they coveted each other, so close, but separated by an invisible cloak of duty and honour — so humbling to watch."

"You are sick!" Willoughby shouted.

"Did you think you could shame me into confession? You cannot touch me, boy, no one can! When Napoleon wins this war, and soon he will, my reward will be great. Mark my words, by autumn we will have an Emperor! He will break the British navy and triumph. And if by any chance he fails, I still have the family's name, land and fortune to protect me."

"He will not succeed. Our navy will break him!"

"Leave me, boy. I will give you a ten minute start. Don't waste them with futile threats!"

Willoughby backed away to the door. He was left with no choice. There was nothing to say, not here, but he would escape, await his time and see justice done. He had never hated anyone so much in his life, not even Spratt. Charles must have been terrified before he died. He was no soldier. And his father had been cheated of his true love and then his life, whilst Nathaniel watched and gloated.

Outside the room, the servant seemed unaware of Willoughby's predicament and showed him courteously to the door. It was opened wide. Willoughby was about to take flight when a gunshot stopped him in his tracks. He stared momentarily at Crombie, and then in unison they ran back inside the study. Nathaniel's body was slumped across his desk where he had been sitting, a pistol held loosely in his hand. In front of him was the letter detailing Charles's death. All the evidence was in place to suggest he had committed suicide.

It made no sense at all to Willoughby.

"Good God, sir. What has he done?" Crombie looked at the blood stained letter on his desk and shook his head, whilst Willoughby stood, taking in every detail of the scene in a room which, moments earlier, had played out a very different scenario.

"The news must have been too much for him. He must have hung on to his despair long enough to inform you, sir. For Lady Rossington's sake, sir, we must see to it that the news of his suicide does not get out. We could assert it was an accident whilst cleaning his gun. He was too noble a gentleman to have such a dishonourable end." Crombie looked cut to the core. "Do you agree, sir?"

"That he was noble?" Willoughby's words nearly stuck in his throat, which Crombie seemed to mistake for raw emotion.

"That it was a travesty, an accident?"

"A true travesty." Willoughby said nothing to challenge the man's assumptions. He looked at the panel directly behind his uncle's desk, facing it, shaken, but then not really surprised. The servant grabbed his arm.

"Would you stay here with Lady Rossington, sir, and make sure that the room is locked? Place the cleaning cloth in his other hand and I'll go and get help."

Willoughby nodded, not able to reply, so lost was he in thought. His family, so honourable for decades, was in disarray. He waited for the man to leave. There was just a hint of the fragrance of lavender in the air. "Aunt," he said softly.

The hidden door behind the desk was opened and his aunt, ashen faced, stepped out. He hugged her; there were a few splashes of blood on her lace gloves. She was in shock; her eyes tight shut seeped tears as he held her frail body in his arms.

"He had my darling Joshua killed ... he sent Charles to his death and he would have had you join them. He watched my love for your father torture us both, and savoured it. Such is the evil of this treacherous man. I lived my life, without love, with a traitor! I had him as a husband! Lain with him... Even I had not realised how low he would sink." Her body sagged as she sobbed.

Swiftly he closed the panel securely leaving no trace of its existence. He put a protective arm around her and half walked, half carried her to the staircase.

"He murdered Joshua. I knew he was cold hearted but this ... I ... not you as well," she was muttering to herself, almost inaudibly.

"Aunt, what you have just done I believe was the only thing that would stop him, and in doing so you have saved even more lives. If only you could have left it to justice and not soiled your own hands with his blood..." Willoughby was whispering back to her, anxious that the servants did not overhear.

"Willoughby, I have lived in hell all my life. If I should die in it too ... then I must. Justice on this earth is non-existent. Pray for me, as if you were a priest ... but I would not let him take you too and I would not have you soil your hands with his blood. You are worth more to me than that." Her moist grey eyes stared into his.

Willoughby held her closely. "You must now go to your room. Give me your gloves. Wash your hands. Take to your bed and let the authorities take care of this. I will have to leave here once things have been seen to, but I shall return. Promise me you will be strong, Aunt Eliza. Promise me! It will be made to look as an accident and you will have to grieve for the husband you have lost. Or appear to have."

"Oh, I know how to grieve, but this time it will not be for his death, it will be for the ones he caused."

"Do not admit to that. I'll have a physician see you, give you something for a grieving widow's nerves, but promise you'll stay up there until all is sorted. I'll not see him destroy you also."

"He did that years ago," she whispered.

"No, you were stronger than he. You did your own work, whilst he used others. Go upstairs and trust me." Willoughby held her hand firmly.

"Yes, yes, I will," she said. "Willoughby, he was sent a note from someone called Francesca. I thought it was his mistress; it said she awaited him in Dover..."

"Don't worry. It will be seen to."

Eliza climbed the stairs, sobbing quietly to herself as she did so. Willoughby summoned one of the housemaids who was starting to appear from the servants' stairs. "Take care of my aunt, she has had a terrible shock," he ordered. "Do not leave her alone. No one must enter Lord Rossington's study. Do you hear me?"

His aunt looked back at him, the pain etched into her face. "You will return, Willoughby, won't you?"

"Yes, Aunt, I give you my word. We will all return to Rossington Hall very soon."

Eliza nodded to him. "You are so like your dear father."

Willoughby saw her safely to the landing, and then made the body look as though Nathaniel had in fact been intending to clean his pistol, before securing the study once more. He then rushed outside to inform Abner. He explained briefly what had happened.

"Leave my horse ready. I will return as soon as I can," Willoughby said. "You go to Beth. I will take her to Kent as soon as I can make arrangements. I will honour my word to her."

Willoughby returned to his uncle's study, removing his keys. Willoughby had set the scene as Crombie had so ingeniously and thoughtfully suggested. When the physician arrived he showed him his uncle's body with the rearranged items surrounding him.

"Very sad! Most distressing. I should like to leave Lady Rossington something to help her sleep and, of course, my condolences. It is quite clear this is an abominable accident." He stared at Willoughby. "You will now be the heir. How, sir, fortune can shine out of misfortune."

"Hardly the time nor place..." Willoughby was genuinely shocked by the comment which pointed out a truth he had not even considered. The title and lands would now come to him.

After two hours Willoughby had found sufficient evidence to incriminate the Inghams, and also to find the papers that showed his uncle owned half the shares in the mine. Nathaniel abhorred weakness, so to have his person referred to in the region as 'Mr King', would humour him. The stain of the contraband would not spill to the Rossington name as he was a sleeping partner, a backer and not involved directly with the business.

He selectively laid out the evidence needed to show the soldiers when they arrived a few hours later. Then, securing the office once more, he said a prayer for the souls of his dead father, uncle and brother, hoping they would now find peace, and then returned to his aunt. Seeing her face, he prayed silently by her bedside. Her life had not been easy, now with blood on her conscience, hell continued for her on earth. Laudanum would help her for the moment.

When the soldiers arrived, Willoughby was half way down the oak staircase making his way to the hall to greet them. The young lieutenant he had met on the moor faced him. "You, sir?"

"I, sir, am..."

"Willoughby James, whom I have been searching for."

"I am Mr Willoughby James Rossington. I had business with Major Husk on behalf of my uncle's office in government. I would have stayed and explained further if perhaps you would have listened to my words without bias. You were seeking the wrong man."

The lieutenant flushed. "I..."

Willoughby stepped down in front of him and offered the man his hand. "I have need of your services in order to arrest the right man ... and woman."

The lieutenant looking relieved nodded, and was shown into the study. "Lieutenant, these documents refer to Mr and Mrs Ingham." Willoughby presented the young soldier with the evidence, as Nathaniel had stated he must. His uncle had been wrong; Willoughby was about to bring justice to his father and succeed. The price, he knew, could now be his aunt's sanity, unless he could find her some peace at last.

# Chapter 23

Willoughby had made sure his aunt was settled before he left with the lieutenant to go to the Ingham's estates. It was quickly determined that, after a life in distinguished service to the country, Lord Rossington died after an unfortunate accident whilst cleaning his pistol. He would be buried, like Charles, with honours. Willoughby had agreed to this version of events, not for the family name, but for his aunt's fragile sanity.

He had stayed long enough to make arrangements for Nathaniel's body to be taken back to London. His aunt would follow with maidservants in the comfort of their coach. The York residence was to be closed.

Beth was relieved to see Abner again. She had been pampered: bathed, changed, fed and left to sleep in a feather bed. Her ordeal with Spratt had been washed away to a bygone place; she felt as if she was starting life anew. With her hair pinned up upon her head except for a few ringlets to frame her small face, she looked pretty and, unusually for Beth, the picture of innocence.

"Well, I seem to have come to the wrong place, miss. I left a frightened young waif here. Have you seen her?" Abner smiled at her as her eyes shone with pride at his compliment.

"She left here, sir, never to be found again. I believe that she was very happy to go."

"Good. Mr Rossington will arrive within the day. After a good meal and a sleep we shall take you to Whitby and set you both on your way to a new life."

"Did he find the man?" Beth asked.

"Oh yes, the problem is resolved and he is no longer hunted. He is free, and you soon will be too." He seated himself on the sofa next to her, and Miss Tully brought in a tray with tea and sweetmeats upon it.

"Will you come with us, Abner?" Beth asked enthusiastically, and caught a flash of concern in Miss Tully's eyes.

"Only as far as Whitby, miss... My life and my heart are here." He glanced at Miss Tully and Beth saw the lady colour slightly. It seemed there was a definite sadness to her features when she heard Abner's response. Beth wondered if it was at the loss of a friend or if the lady had actual desires for him.

They made an odd combination, the two of them, but they were well suited in temperament: one strong, bold and confident, the other genteel and graceful. Beth hoped beyond hope that when Willoughby arrived she would impress him as much, for as she was, she did not look like a down-trodden girl, but a young woman ready to blossom in the world. They were moving away from her memories, from her past and she hoped he would, in time, forget them, although she knew he had a lot to forget about how he found her.

Willoughby and the young lieutenant were accepted into the Ingham household and shown into the drawing room, where Mr and Mrs Ingham were seated.

"Rossington..." Mrs Ingham said rather loudly.

Her husband looked at her. "Whatever is it? Do these people disturb you, my dear? Why so?"

"We shall be disturbing you greatly, Mr Ingham, I am afraid, as we have some sad news. Firstly, Lord Nathaniel Rossington is dead..."

The man gasped. "Good God, man, my business is half owned by him." He had the good grace to look genuinely shocked. "Was it a sudden illness?" he asked, but Willoughby's eyes were fixed on Simone Ingham, who stared knowingly back into his.

"Why come all this way to inform us personally? It is a waste of your effort and time, and we are not prepared to receive visitors." Simone sniffed, dabbed her eyes with her lace kerchief and glanced down. "Poor man, and yet relatively young still. My condolences to you and Lady Rossington." She looked at Willoughby. "Dead," she whispered, "such a final word."

Willoughby walked over to her. "Joshua was murdered five years ago, but you know that. Lord Nathaniel Rossington, my uncle, died yesterday evening. He left a list of names and proof that he had been accumulating regarding traitors operating for Napoleon along this shore."

Mrs Ingham gasped and covered her throat with her left hand whilst her husband held her other one.

"There is nowhere safe in this world anymore," Roderick Ingham remarked calmly.

"Indeed not, sir," Willoughby agreed. "We can even have them within our own circle and not suspect it." He stared at Simone Ingham.

Her eyes met his with icy determination. "I don't know what you are inferring, young man, but I think you should both go. I thank you for bringing us this sad news personally and offer my condolences," Mr Ingham replied.

"We wish to interview your wife at the fort, Mr Ingham. She has been implicated and we have proof of her involvement, both in the current situation and in the affair she had with my father, which resulted in his murder."

She stood up. "This is an outrage!"

Roderick Ingham looked at her, dumbstruck.

"You can't believe this! It is lies, Roderick. I told you the truth. You must stop them from saying such things... Roderick..." Simone stared at her husband who had let go of her hand and was standing by the fireside, his back turned to her.

"You have proof, you say, of espionage?" He was looking at Willoughby.

"We recovered papers from my uncle's study and also from that of Major Husk that link times and dates with Simone Ingham's name along with the arrangements of transfers of sums of money, bonds and jewellery between venues as payment... We have no doubts."

Simone turned and tried to run for the doors at the opposite end of the room. It was her husband who brought her down with one strike from the poker which he grabbed from the stand at the side of the fire.

She groaned. He did not even stay to see how badly she was injured.

"You must excuse me gentlemen, I have business in London. You can contact me there at my house in Mayfair. I will leave the card of my legal representatives. The whore will answer all your questions. I will divorce her as soon as it is possible, for she has betrayed me and the Ingham name also. I have nothing to answer for."

He took a step forward to be blocked by the lieutenant.

"Indeed you do, sir. We are currently searching your docked vessels and your office. There are charges of smuggling to answer." The lieutenant signalled to his men who swiftly took him outside to the waiting carriage, ignoring his protestations of innocence.

Willoughby knelt down by the weeping woman.

"I loved him; he was too good to work for Nathaniel. Joshua realised it was the two of us together, but much too late."

"N to S," Willoughby said and helped her stand, "Nathaniel to Simone."

"Let me go, Willoughby, let me be free. For him. He loved me; he would not want this for me…"

"You are as guilty as the man who pushed my father from the headland, Simone. You will answer for your treachery, for he loved you and you betrayed him as you did this country." He walked her outside to the carriage and helped her climb inside.

Willoughby mounted his horse and made ready to leave. The coach moved at a gentle pace down the drive, slowing as it turned between the avenues of trees that sheltered Upthorpe Hall from the north-easterly winds.

Willoughby heard Mr Ingham shout out; he rode around the other side of the coach just in time to see Mrs Ingham broken loose and hesitating at the edge of the cliffs.

"Do you really want to do this, Lady Ingham?" he shouted.

"Your presence brought Joshua back to me, Willoughby."

A soldier dismounted and ran two steps towards her, but she turned, screaming, as she threw herself bodily over the edge.

Willoughby stared at Mr Ingham who looked back at him seemingly unperturbed. "It was her. I am a wronged man. Her cowardly act proves it."

"Onwards," the lieutenant ordered.

The coach increased its speed and the soldiers rode with it. The lieutenant saluted Willoughby.

"I must go my own way, lieutenant. When you have dealt with these, go to the orphanage in York and arrest a man named Gilbert, who sells on the orphans."

"Very well, sir." The soldier nodded.

Willoughby took the coastal road back towards Ebton, hopefully to find some fresh air. Ingham would perish.

# Chapter 24

Hearing the sea roaring from below as he followed the coastal path by the wall, he felt an eerie awareness of Simone Ingham's watery grave, a re-enactment of his father's own murder. He had had enough of death. Lovers in life, betrayers both — his father to his mother and the Ingham wench to her husband, her adoptive country and to the man she professed to have loved. They were both now dead. He stared out to sea. The time of mourning for the last five years without his father would soon be over. His uncle's funeral, hypocritical as the service would be, would be an end to the Rossington Rot, as he saw it. He would carve out a future for their name which returned honour to it. He would obey no man. His fortune would be used to help right the wrongs.

Retribution had been made, and for those who still walked this earth, justice would now be given as they were rounded up for offences from smuggling to common assault.

The inn where Spratt had left this world was ahead of him. He kicked his horse onwards. He had no wish to pass directly in front of it. Willoughby knew ghosts could not harm him, but Spratt had accomplices, and their world had been thrown into turmoil. They would be facing a harsher and poorer existence until they managed to build up their own contacts and hierarchy again if they survived the hunt. The trade would increase eventually; he was not naive enough to think they could eradicate it altogether, unless Napoleon was beaten.

Willoughby had to cross over farmland in order to avoid the inn itself, but as the road took him onto Stangcliffe, he glanced back and saw two men bringing a third horse to the back of the building. He paused for a few moments, watching.

Some time passed before a third man joined them. He was either old or injured as they helped him onto the horse. He was dressed in a fisherman's coat and wool hat by the look, but... Willoughby froze. He did not know if it could be. How dead was Spratt before Beth escaped? His hand gripped the reins of his horse tightly. The man, of wiry frame, was clinging to the horse for dear life as they made their way up the tracks to the main moor road.

He knew Abner would still be in Ebton. He had said he would see Burdon, and then collect Beth there, so together they would complete the journey back to Whitby, and board a ship to London. London would need to know the traitor had died, the plans were returned and a ring smashed. However, no one would be given the name Rossington. The Inghams would take the blame, the traitoress dead and the smuggler imprisoned or transported.

Willoughby galloped as if he wanted the horse to take flight. He had to get help. Praying Burdon was there, he headed straight for the vicarage.


Willoughby saw the riders in the distance change direction. Instead of heading south they too were riding north, and then branching towards the coastal path. From the headland he looked down to the small hamlet of Ebton, nestled in the bay. They were riding past the top of the gill where the millwheel slowly turned, making towards the old Norman church. This small enclave had only one path leading from it that would lead to the vicarage on the edge of Ebton. He galloped with the wind behind him as fast as possible along the track. If the Reverend Burdon was at home, he appeared to be their first target — or contact?

Willoughby left his horse outside the graveyard and climbed over the wall. His pistol was loaded and in his hand. He ran across to the vicarage in the evening shadows of the church. There was a light flickering in the reverend's study. Willoughby made straight for the vicarage and tapped on the small panelled window. Sleepily the reverend opened it.

"The door is the usual point of entry, Willoughby," he remarked, but his eyes were scouting the land behind Willoughby looking for trouble.

"Get your coat and gun and leave now. Spratt and his men will arrive shortly."

"But he's dead, you said…"

"Move, I'll get Abner, meet me at the cottage. Explain to no one."

"Abner won't be there. Wait for me, I'll show you where the girl is." Within minutes the reverend was leaving the vicarage and running across the graveyard with Willoughby. They were almost to the wall when three riders arrived at the lych gate. Quickly, they both crouched low to the ground, hiding behind headstones, hidden by the shadows.

Two men dismounted and ran up to the vicarage door. The groundsman and his wife, the reverend's own housekeeper, greeted them, then ran down the path to support the wiry frame of Spratt, who was clearly unsteady on his feet.

"'Tis the best place for ghosts, I suppose. What do you say?" the reverend quipped.

"No, but it is a great place for a body," Willoughby snapped the words out under his breath.

"You would murder him, here?" the reverend gasped. "Willoughby, think of the stain upon your hands…"

"No, I would not, although he deserves it. Such an act would start a battle that we cannot win. It would appear the three are now five. How long have your staff been in their ring?" he whispered.

"Two years — since I have been here. I knew it, but better to work with them under my watch, than turn them out and have them as enemies. This has been an insular community for generations. It is only as the roads are improved and new houses are built that they are having to accept strangers. By the time their grandchildren are born they may be considered local. Such is the speed of change here."

"You must take me to Abner, for Beth is not safe and we must not let Spratt get her before we can nab him. Tonight the man must be caught. His time is up. He has killed his last victim and hurt his last girl." Willoughby tapped the man's shoulder and gestured to the wall. "Quickly now, up and over it, my horse is waiting."

# Chapter 25

Burdon showed him the way through the shadows, behind cottages and shrubbery, until they were near the new buildings. Then Burdon ran around the back and let himself in the unlocked door.

"Bolt it!" Willoughby said. Both he and Burdon entered Miss Tully's home. The lady was ready to retire. She had no servant living there as Burdon understood that she liked her privacy. Abner was standing in the hallway behind her.

"Reverend..." She looked startled as the two men pushed their way in quickly after securing the door behind them. Hopefully no one had seen them enter from the village below.

"Miss Tully," Willoughby began, and nodded an acknowledgement of Abner. "We are sorry to burst in like this, but we need to move Beth. I've seen Spratt's men combing the area."

"Then she will be safe here," Abner replied. "She's Miss Millicent now."

"No, I'm afraid not, Abner. You see they know you will be hiding her as she was seen at the vicarage, and my staff know where you live in the village. I am afraid they will tell him that I left the girl with you." The reverend looked at Abner directly.

"He is dead, Spratt, isn't he?" Abner looked to Willoughby, but Willoughby's attention had been distracted by the vision of a young woman, groomed, pretty and pale, as her hand went to her neck and she stared back into his eyes, shaking her head. Beth's nightmare had just returned.

Willoughby heard Beth take in a quick breath. "I didn't hit him hard enough, did I? There was so much blood. He was so limp. I thought he was dead."

Willoughby put his arm out to her and, without hesitation, Beth ran to him.

"I think not," he said as he gently held her to him.

Abner pulled on his greatcoat and picked up his rifle. "Come, miss, wear your coat and we shall take you across the marshes to my boat."

"Boat?" Beth repeated.

"Aye, without it we would have to swim, because there is no way we can get you out by the only road in and out of this place. It would be an ambush, a death trap, and no one would have seen or heard a thing. People would bolt their doors, turn the other way and deny they heard anything above the noise of the ocean."

"You take her, Abner. I have business to finish here, and then I shall join you in Whitby. Reverend, do you wish to go with them?" Willoughby asked.

"I shall stay with you. It will be an unenviable task; you cannot take them on your own, even a limping man is better than none. You have no local knowledge and do not think like they do. I have and do."

Abner put a hand on Willoughby's shoulder. "Come with us. You will die this night if you do not. This is their territory. You stand no chance. Never fear, your chance will come soon enough. The hound will follow our trail to Whitby. From there we can get Beth away, and then I promise you, together we will finish what we have started. Besides, it is a heavy sea and I'll need your strength or we will not get far."

Willoughby looked down at the frightened eyes of Beth.

"Please, Willoughby, stay with me. You need me to keep you safe," she said and forced a smile upon her trembling lips.

Despite his desire to hunt the man down once and for all, he knew they spoke sense. He looked at Abner, and then to the reverend.

"He speaks sense," the man admitted.

Willoughby nodded, putting anger aside and listening to common sense. "Lead the way."

Beth rushed to retrieve her coat. Abner produced a black scarf from his pocket. "Wrap this around your head, girl, or your pale face will light our way and show them their trail."

Miss Tully called to Abner. He quickly ran up the stairs two at a time. The group looked uncomfortable.

"I will sell up here, Abner. Leave word where you go, for you will not be able to return... If they suspect that you helped them, then..."

"Not now, Lizzy. I will send word, no need to fret."

They extinguished the lamp and, in silence, slipped back out into the darkness of night. Abner walked the horse along to a piece of rough grass away from the house and then led them onto a sandy, damp track which cut around and across the open expanse of marshes.

After walking and stumbling for some time, they came to a broad row of sand dunes. Beth's feet slipped from under her a few times as the soft sand gave way, her hands occasionally poked by the sharp edges of marram grass as she made her way up and down the winding path. She found herself bodily lifted up between Willoughby and Abner on a few occasions as if her two guardian angels had given her wings. Eventually, they came out onto the flat sand of the bay. Willoughby scooped Beth in his arm and guided her against the wind, which blew directly in over the waves that crashed on the shore.

Abner pointed down the beach to where the shape of a boat could just be made out.

"We run together for it. Here we are exposed. Even in the dark, a trained eye can catch movement. The tide is out. Grab a side of the boat and together we will drag it the few yards to the sea. Beth, you'll clamber in as soon as we meet the shoreline and look after the guns. Make sure they don't fall in the water. Reverend, Willoughby, we will push the boat beyond the breakers and climb in. Reverend, you will be first in, you next," he looked at Willoughby, "then me. We will, God willing, get clean away before they discover our tracks."

"I've never been in a boat before," Beth admitted.

"What would you rather face, the sea and adventure, or an irate Oberon Spratt?"

"What are we waiting for?" she asked.

Willoughby grinned at her; she was so scared she was trembling, but she was determined to try and hide it.

"Now!" Abner said. All four broke into a run. They managed to reach the boat before the distant crack of a musket firing urged them to speed up and increase their efforts, and grab hold of the coble, the local style of flat-bottomed boat.

# Chapter 26

Willoughby pulled on the oar in unison with Abner. The reverend and Beth sat behind them trying with all their might to add their limited strength to that of the two stronger men. In the distance, flames shot up into the sky. The village was illuminated and figures could be seen running back and fore.

The boat lurched one way then the next. One minute they stared at a mass of water, the next, as they headed around Stangcliffe and along the coast, they could see the land. Willoughby loved the fleeting feeling of freedom, knowing that Spratt and his men could not reach Beth here. However, he looked at Abner and saw the man's face was moist with more than the spray of the waves. Abner glanced across as he was obviously fighting back tears, and pulled angrily on the oar.

"Is it your cottage that is burning?" Willoughby shouted across to him.

Abner nodded and cleared his throat. "More than that, white man, it is my life going up in flames. Spratt has declared war. There is no easy place for a black man to hide on these shores once an enemy like him has your name written on his slate. He once freed me. Now he has condemned me in my absence. We better lay a careful trap for him, or his shadow will remain over us for life."

"You will make a new start. You can rebuild it, once Spratt is caught," Willoughby said as they had cusped the next swell of the mass of water. Beth squealed as they slipped down sideways, into the darkness.

"You couldn't understand. They will never have me back here. I can never have a home here again and, as for Miss

Tully... My name has been damned by them. She would not be safe working with me. Spratt will die for this. I will crush his skull as he has my heart. Don't worry, Rossington, your hands will not be soiled."

They had to work hard to pass Stangcliffe, the first of the headlands and bay towns. All their energy was needed to take them to Whitby. The horizon was a mass of shipping, the colliers, the alum ships and the odd fishing boat all following their trades.

Beth coped well, clinging on from the buffeting they constantly fought through the water. Willoughby braced himself against the breakers as they finally approached the open harbour of Whitby.

"We will beach it before we reach the harbour. I don't want anyone announcing our arrival." Abner pointed to a flat sandy stretch of coast and a little inlet. "There, we go there. Stay quiet. Sounds travel, even on a wave swept shoreline. Those used to the sounds of the sea can blot them out and hear only the noises that are different, believe me. These shores have a secret life of their own."

Willoughby nodded and could see a change in Abner. The man had taken on an emotionless sheen that seemed to spread out over him. It was more powerful than the open anger he had expressed earlier. This was thinly controlled rage; the rage of a man who did not care if he survived as long as revenge was his first.

Willoughby and Abner jumped out of the boat into the shallow waves and pulled the vessel ashore. As Beth was lifted out, Abner paused and pointed to the sea. Turning on the horizon he could just make out a coble with at least eight men pulling hard, heading towards their landing place.

"Reverend, we best run." Abner led the way. They crossed the flat sand, but instead of taking to the streets Abner showed them the entrance to a low tunnel. "In here!"

"God in his Heaven must truly look down on you kindly! Could you not have found a place more unlikely, man?"

Abner ignored the priest's comments and after twenty paces changed direction, leading them out onto the street and, without explanation, he ran across the wooden bridge to the abbey side of the Esk. When they had all safely crossed they stopped to catch their breath at the end of an old snicket.

"Explain," Willoughby said.

"Leticia Gill was married to a man who died suddenly — uncommonly suddenly. Her husband worked as an excise officer, her brother is a soldier, a lieutenant. She is a woman not to be messed with. She lives a quiet life here in Whitby and is a friend of Miss Tully; that suits us both well, or did!" Abner explained.

They saw figures appearing from the alleys across the river.

"Come," Abner said, and they ran as quickly as they could to a shop front.

The door was locked.

The reverend was about to knock on it.

"No! You'll wake the whole street, Mr Burdon," Beth whispered and looked down to the right and saw a hatch to a cellar. "Abner, force that open and I'll climb down ... hurry."

Within minutes she was feeling around in the dark, inside the cold cellar. She shivered, but realised it was because of the memory of Spratt. He wasn't dead. Now the spectre was haunting her and threatening her life again and her future with Mr Willoughby. Willoughby had seen her washed and dressed as a lady and had smiled. He would smile like that at her again, she promised, as she fumbled in the dark. His arms had been warm, comforting and strong, and being so close to his heart had triggered something within her own. Somehow, Willoughby would be hers. Spratt must die. She must live.

Beth managed to force her way into the shop and then opened the door. She was greeted with a harsh push in the back and was about to be beaten with a rolling pin when the lantern was lit by a woman and Abner's voice was heard demanding, "Stop!"

Mrs Leticia Gill put down the pin. Beth, without explanation, let the weary, wet men inside. She shut the door firmly.

"Abner, go secure the cellar. Take this." Beth took the lamp and gave it to him. He nodded and squeezed through the narrow hatch to the room below.

"Would someone mind explaining to me what on earth this invasion of my property is in aid of? This is my home, not a hideout for the destitute!" Mrs Leticia Gill stood firm, arms crossed in front of her.

Willoughby placed his hand on Beth's shoulder. "Can we take our conversation into the back room?" They walked through. "We are being hunted, madam. Beth is in grave danger and we need somewhere for her to stay until we can leave on a passage to London." Willoughby saw the face of Leticia harden.

"Who is hunting her?"

"A man called Oberon Spratt." Willoughby looked at the Reverend Burdon, who appeared to be distracted.

"Spratt! You've brought Oberon Spratt to my door? He brought down my husband. My brother risks his life determined to find him and bring him to justice, and I seek to have a life free of him and the misery he causes." She walked up to him and prodded him hard in his chest. "What right do you have to bring so much trouble to my home? Has it not had enough, priest?" She looked to Burdon.

Willoughby thought of the young lieutenant eager to make his mark, and was amazed as he connected the two characters, because he was so like his sister in looks, if not in attitude. Before Willoughby could speak, the reverend interrupted, "Excuse me, ma'am, but isn't Abner taking a long time just to secure a hatch?"

Willoughby stepped around Mrs Gill and, with pistol in hand, went down to the cellar. He returned within minutes.

"It would appear that we have an added problem. He seems to have left us. I suspect he has gone for Spratt on his own."

# Chapter 27

"I think we could all do with a drink," Reverend Burdon said.

"Oh, I'll make one shall I?" Leticia snapped.

"Thank you. I'd really appreciate it," he said, without acknowledging the woman's sarcasm.

"I should go and look for him," Willoughby said.

Beth looked at Mrs Gill. "I'll make the drink if you want to join them, Mrs."

Leticia looked down at Beth and shook her head. "No, lass. I'll do it. Pride comes afore a fall and I've had enough excitement tonight." She looked at Willoughby. "I'll go to the fort in the morning and arrange for my brother to sort a safe transport for you and the girl to go to London, if it is your wish."

"Yes, it is. I shall find Abner first, though..." Willoughby persisted as he headed for the door.

"No, you won't. He has murder on his mind and you do not want blood on your hands too. See to this girl. Make her safe. Let my brother and your man, Abner, sort out the dross. You have done enough. Be content to still have your lives."

"Mr Willoughby, if you goes, you won't come back. They crawl these streets like rats. I don't want Abner hurt, but he is strong. You wait, cos Spratt will come for us. So let him. On your own soil, where you have the upper hand... Please."

Willoughby nodded and Beth openly hugged him. He would have to meet up with his aunt, but he would see Beth safe this time.

The next morning, Willoughby persuaded Mrs Leticia Gill that he should accompany her to see the Lieutenant at the barracks.

Mrs Gill's persistent manner impressed Willoughby as she explained to the soldier at the gate that she wished to see her brother, right away. He tried not to smile as they were escorted to a small room in the gatehouse. A few moments later, Lieutenant Gill called them inside his office and dismissed the soldier.

"We meet again," he said to Willoughby and then glanced at his sister who stood pursing her lips. "Leticia what do you mean by presenting yourself here? Could you not have sent word?" He stood before her and removed his hat, placing it on the small table.

"I am pleased to see you too, Percival!" she snapped back at him.

He glanced at Willoughby and sighed. "What is the problem now?" he asked him.

Before Willoughby could reply his sister explained.

"I have visitors, Percival; uninvited, and definitely not wanted. However, they need your help. I believe you are acquainted with Mr Rossington here. He has a young woman with him who is being chased by the man, Oberon Spratt."

"Spratt? My sergeant thinks he may have found one of his men. He's in a bad way, been beaten up, a black."

"Is he badly injured?" Willoughby asked. "I know the man and can speak for him. He is not one of Spratt's men."

"He will ache for days, but he is not broken, no."

"You must treat him well, Percival. You will have to arrange an escort to get Mr Rossington, his ward Elizabeth and this man, Abner, to safety. They want to travel to London. Firstly, though, you will need to bring them here. I have no room for them to stay in my home and I do not want them seen being harboured there. It would not do my reputation any good."

"I dearly would appreciate your help in this, Lieutenant," Willoughby added, and was relieved when the man opposite nodded his agreement.

Lt. Gill answered his sister directly. "Don't worry, Leticia. I will have you escorted back in the covered wagon. You slip into your home and have Elizabeth slip back out. I'll have this 'Abner' fellow moved from the cells to a room and have him treated well, if you say he is deserving of such care."

# Chapter 28

Mrs Gill made arrangements for them to sail on a vessel bound for London the next day. Their journey would be straight from Whitby's busy harbour to the Thames and their first destination, London. When Abner returned, he was given no reasonable choice, when he complained bitterly as he still wanted to find Spratt. Either he was to be arrested for smuggling, handling and distributing contraband, or go with Rossington.

They travelled upon a packet to the Thames. Abner was hustled into a carriage with Beth, which only stopped when it reached the address Willoughby had given to the driver. Beth looked to her new friend and saw his clenched fist still at his side. "Stop hating, Abner, it does you no good."

"I will find him, Millicent ... Beth. I will make him pay and I must make sure that Miss Tully is well and that she understands that I will never be allowed to live amongst the villagers again. Once they close ranks on you, you're as good as dead." He stared out of the coach's window.

"If Spratt is alive after the trouble that me and Mr Willoughby have caused him, don't worry, he'll find us wherever we hide." She stroked his bruised cheek gently. "You get strong again and wait for him to come. He will. He always does. I know we'll need your strength, Abner — your character, not just muscle. Mr Willoughby is a true gentleman. He's good in a fair fight, but Spratt don't play fair. He's scum, and you and me, we understand scum. Mr Willoughby will need us both to be watchful."

Willoughby had seated himself atop the coach with the driver. He had made two stops along the way: one at a bank, one by a government office.

"Beth, Mr Willoughby is not as helpless as you think he is. I think you see him through biased vision. Believe me, girl, gentlemen can fight dirty."

Willoughby, watchful, climbed down and opened the carriage door for his two friends. Two footmen appeared behind him and helped Abner in, Beth following on behind. They took him up the stairs leading to the bedchambers. Willoughby entered one and a servant brought in fresh water.

"Jeffries, send for my tailor; tell him I'll need a friend outfitted and he will have five days in which to do it. Tell Mary to organise two hot tubs: one in my own room and one for my friend here. He may need some of Cook's healing balm also."

Abner, who was spread out on a chaise longue, waited for Jeffries to leave. "Do I have any say in this or have you taken over control of my life, sir?"

"Abner, you can leave now, but you would never see Spratt brought to justice if you do, because it is myself and Beth he will seek out. You might die trying to do it yourself, or be whisked away on board one of the other types of ships we passed and smelt in the docks. Stay with us, become strong in body and soul, and come with me to my estate in Kent. I need you to protect Beth whilst I see to my uncle's affairs and my aunt's welfare. There are greater issues here than our personal revenge. The nation's security was breached. I have to report in, properly. Trust me as I have you."

Abner leaned forward. "Miss Tully..."

"Before I left, I asked Reverend Burdon to deliver a message to her. She will be safe. I will make sure of it. Abner, I need you strong and in control. We have a journey to complete, and whilst I am away, I want you with Beth. Have faith! If you wish, I will write a note for you and make sure Miss Tully receives it."

"Provide paper, quill and ink and I will write it myself!"

"Yes, Abner, I will provide them... I apologise, I should have realised you were capable of this." The empty tub was carried in and placed before the newly lit fire. He turned to Abner. "Stay with us please?"

Abner nodded, but the hatred which burned in his heart was almost palpable.

Willoughby found Beth sitting staring out of a window, lost to thought. "Come, Beth, I shall introduce you to a lady friend of mine. You will spend the time with her. She owns the property a few doors down the Crescent. I am afraid I know few dressmakers."

Beth was transported from her impoverished and desperate past to a life she could never have imagined. In a fashionable area of London, she was roomed with a respectable lady. In the few weeks she was there, she was given more garments to wear than she knew what to do with. The lady was quite severe in manner, but patient with her at the same time. She was shown what to wear and when. New clothes filled her own trunk; it was what she imagined heaven to be like. New foods were introduced to her — sweetmeats — and fine wine and table manners were some of the things to learn and remember along with a myriad of delicacies to eat. A new word 'etiquette' represented a challenge to her simple ways. Beth knew she would only be there for a short time as Willoughby saw to his uncle's affairs, but she didn't want it to end. Her dream of riding in a fine coach had come true. She wanted now to have her other dream fulfilled. She wanted to be Willoughby's lady. Her heart was so happy that she thought it would burst with the joy she felt. Only one shadow clouded her bliss and that was of Mr Oberon Spratt. She felt his hatred, knew he would appear, but, as the days passed by, in this strange world full of servants and luxuries, even his threat had diminished.

From her bedroom window, she could see the fine carriages with the ladies inside, fine people promenading through the park opposite and young rakes riding their fine horses, catching the ladies' eye. She imagined herself and Mr Willoughby walking arm in arm. If only she could change what had been. If only he could forget that and in time look upon her as his lover. If only...

Beth revelled in the opportunity to learn new things — as well as the attention. Learning how to wear one's hair, after it had been nearly pulled out as it had been washed, oiled, combed, washed again and brushed until the lady thought it clean enough and controlled enough to be dressed and redressed was a fine example. In the time she spent with this lady, rising early, going to bed late, she had come to believe herself to be a young lady suitable to be the ward of a fine gentleman like Mr Willoughby James Rossington — for the time being — whilst she impressed him and he learned to love her.

It was only at night time as she stood wearing her petticoat, admiring her fuller curves and her new healthy glow, that a shadow crossed her mind of a time when she had stood before a man in a tricorn hat, naked and scrawny. She saw goose bumps rise on her skin. She'd thought she had killed him ... thought she had needed to, but she felt the fear again. Beth knew Oberon would find her whilst he still had a breath left in his body. Nobody crossed him and lived. Beth had nearly destroyed him and in the process destroyed his empire. She glanced around at her finery and wiped a tear from her face as she curled up into a ball on the large feather bed. Now she had so much; the more she had, the more she had to lose: all this and a lifetime with her Mr Willoughby.

Willoughby found his aunt was not still lying abed, but instead she had begun arising, ready for the day. Dressed in a mourning gown, she was seated in the day room, working her embroidery. In her sombre attire, she looked like a shadow of her former self. However, her face lit up the moment he entered.

"You look tired, Willoughby. Come rest with me, you spend too much time careering around and not enough reflecting on your life and future. After the funeral you must stay a while." Her voice was shaky, polite, guarded.

"Aunt, I want you to return to Kent with me." He seated himself in the chair opposite and saw her hands were even less steady than her voice appeared to be.

"That would be splendid, Willoughby, dear. When shall we go? I will need time to organise closing the house up." She put down her embroidery and placed her hands on her lap, toying slightly with her lace gloves.

"I have to tie up a few loose ends first, but you can organise the servants to close up this house as you wish, Aunt. The house in York will be sold and we all need to retire to Kent to rest and recover."

"Always loose ends! Always another journey, Willoughby ... always more danger!" Her mood changed and her temper snapped. "What if I don't want to sell it?"

"Then I would not insist that you did, but, Aunt, it is not a home, it is a place where Uncle's duties were organised. It was never your home. Kent and the London houses are, and the memories of what happened there will do you harm. Besides, I have the legal right to if I wished, now."

"I am aware of how much my future now depends upon the whim of yet another man, even a good one. One who knows the truth about his aunt: her love for his father and the blood upon her hands. Harm? You think I fear ghosts? You think I fear death? No, my young man, I fear life, what little I have left. I cannot live my life again. It was stolen from me when I was a naïve little fool, as was my love. No, I do not fear death; I have learnt to live within it most of my life."

"Then let it go, the house. Come with me — us. Discover life again. Enjoy whatever is left of it." He had knelt by her. "Aunt, breathe in the fresh sea air. Love the moment, make your own choices and be free. You will have the means given to you to do so. I will not put restraints upon you."

"I murdered him, Willoughby; I have no right to enjoy anything. I don't regret it, not after what he had done to his own family, but how can you look at me and touch me and... How can I sit in church and listen to all the lies they will say about him and before God, ask for forgiveness, or grieve... Willoughby, I can't do it."

"You won't have to. You will not be there. It is not your place. I will, and you will be on your way to Kent with a companion at your side. You have always been my rock. You must live with this, but I'll not judge or condemn you. We shall not be alone. There is a young woman who needs your guidance, a man who has a forbidden love, and I hope that the lady in question will join you as a companion and teach the woman, Elizabeth, how to be a lady. It shall not be dull, Aunt." Her head turned to face his.

"How busy you have been. And do these people know the truth? Do they blackmail you, Willoughby, to buy their silence and protect me?"

"No! They are friends. They were hurt by a man who worked for uncle. They are lost souls, as are we. Aunt, our family is seen as noble and heroic, when in fact it has been destroyed from within. I will need time to rebuild it and also you will need a distraction. Elizabeth is very distracting, but I hope you become fond of her character." He smiled.

"And you, what of your future? Surely you are not having feelings for this 'Elizabeth'? You are a lord now. The title, the property shall all be yours. You will need to find a 'lady' of some means to match you." She stopped talking as he stood and looked at her.

"I will not be 'matched'. We have more than enough wealth. I will not become a Nathaniel or a Jeremiah. My name is Willoughby James, in my mind, until I can decide to accept 'Rossington' as a name to be proud of again. So allow me also to adjust. I will go where I am needed, but for now, I will enjoy just being settled and putting the estate in order." Willoughby saw her staring at him, wanting to ask more questions, but acting upon discretion. "Don't even think of asking, Aunt Eliza, I need time too. Our lives will not be the same again. Never will they be predictable. Now, you have a house to organise and a guest to care for whilst I see to the formalities." He smiled, before leaving her to her thoughts once more.

# Chapter 29

*One month later*

Beth laughed, an infectious giggle, as she ran barefoot through the edge of the froth of breaking waves. She held her skirt high as the water almost reached her knees. Deciding she had pushed her luck as far as she dare today, she ran back onto the fine sand.

Willoughby shook his head at her. In his white shirt which billowed with the breeze about his muscular frame, casually wearing breeches and boots, he held her boots and stockings in his hand as he wandered along the shoreline. This was Rossington land, a private bay, which was only overlooked by a steep coastal path. He had played here as a boy and knew how to find his way up and down the cliff edge. Smugglers had used this cove, landing and stashing contraband. He'd known that, because he'd watched them. It was his knowledge that had shown the revenue officer how to catch the man's prey. He would not have told on the odd local fisherman out to make an easier living for his family, but when a gang grew menacing, controlling the locals and delivering its own justice, then it had to be stopped. The result was the breaking of Solomon Able Spratt and his scum, Barnabas Spratt had escaped the rope and been transported instead. The lad Oberon had escaped justice only to survive and recreate hell elsewhere. His smile faltered at the memory of the name. He must have had someone's help. That person was Nathaniel, who had saved and groomed the desperate Oberon.

"Beth, you are either a free spirit or a hopeless case for womanhood. Hasn't my aunt or Miss Tully told you how a young lady should behave?" He washed his thoughts away as usual by breathing in the sheer joy and energy Beth had brought to his life.

"I reckon, but with just you here, I don't have to pretend to anyone, do I?" She took her stockings from him and sat upon a rock.

"No, Beth, that you do not."

"Call me Elizabeth, please?" She giggled, "I love the way your lordship says the word. It rolls off your tongue like honey."

"Elizabeth, you have a fanciful nature." He watched her futile efforts as she tried to brush off the sand from her feet and ankles. "To me you shall always be my Beth. Here," he untucked the end of his shirt from his breeches and used the dry fabric to flick the grains of sand from Beth's feet. It was as he did this that he saw the look in her eyes, and realised as he stroked her naked ankle that this woman who he had found trapped in an inn, now looked happy and healthy in both mind and body. He looked into those eyes, hopeful, inviting, nervous, and saw one unmistakable emotion — love. How blind could he have been?

He slipped her stocking over her toes, along her foot to her ankle, and then flicked the sand from the other foot, repeating the process. "Now, pull them up and cover yourself up, woman. I'll give you a piggy back to the path and you can put your boots back on there."

Quickly she did as she was told. Clinging onto Willoughby's back, she laughed continuously. Willoughby loved being with her, so refreshing she was from the propriety of life with his aunt. The woman had grown fond of Beth, yet he suspected it was not acceptance, but more of the way one would adopt a puppy as a companion or play thing. He knew their situation could not last, but had decided they both deserved some enjoyment from life before life changed again. He placed her down carefully onto the path. She leaned on him as she struggled to pull on her boots. Once her boots were secured he found himself still holding on to her sides. Instinctively, she hugged him. He placed a hand gently on her head. She squeezed him to her and looked up into his face.

"What are we to do, Beth?" he said softly.

Her answer was a gentle kiss on his lips. Willoughby was surprised to find that he responded. She stepped onto a small rock and, what had started as an innocent kiss, became a full passionate embrace lasting minutes as they probed and explored the emotion and passion of the moment, completely lost to time.

When the kiss ended, they stepped apart; both stared at each other, bewildered.

"Beth ... I..."

"Don't, Mr Willoughby, I know. I understand how it is. I cannot erase my past. No one ever kissed me like that before, though. You are special, Mr Willoughby. You make me feel..." Without adding more she ran two steps up the path. "You'll make some virgin a great husband. Come on, don't spoil the day. I've me reading to do."

He shook his head. How crude she was and, he realised, how right also. She was smiling as she made her way up; her endless chatter continued unabated, talking of everything and nothing at the same time. However, Willoughby knew her past was not of her making, but could he forget it? Was he man enough to? Did he want to? He followed on behind, lost to his thoughts, aware of the noise of the breaking waves below, but lost so much to his inner turmoil that he had failed to notice the cessation of her voice as he reached the top path. It was only as Willoughby stepped onto the open headland that he snapped out of his thoughts as the past came back to haunt both of them again.

# Chapter 30

Spratt had grabbed Beth and pulled her in front of him across the saddle of his horse. The barrel of his pistol was pressed into the nape of her neck.

Willoughby had nothing he could grab to defend her, nowhere he could run and no way of reaching the horse. He'd promised to protect her, told her she would be safe here with him.

"What, priest, no sermons? Nothing to say? No words of humility to try to appeal to my better nature? I'm disappointed in you." He kept the horse steady, a clear ten feet from where Willoughby stood.

"It is me you want, Spratt. Release the girl." Willoughby knew it was a futile request, but he needed time.

"Don't flatter yourself. You are as insignificant as your father before you. In fact, I have watched you for days, waiting to find the right time and place for you to join him. It would appear that the time has arrived, the place is perfect!" Spratt moved the horse forward a pace.

Willoughby stared down the cliff at the steep drop. The tide was out; he could see sand and rocks. He looked back to Beth's tear stained face. "Name your price!" he shouted into the wind.

"I am about to put your faith back in humankind, Rossington. Money cannot buy me. I shall rise above such a low attempt to corrupt me from my duty, for I do not need your fraternity. Your uncle paid me well enough; my father's legacy plus my own business acumen has given me sufficient funds to retire on. In fact, Beth and I will retire together on it."

"I have plans, you see. Bonds bought, and a new start for us both in the colonies away from traitors. See me brother, Barnabas. She'll enjoy him."

Willoughby took a step forward.

"So you have no intention of blowing her brains out then?"

He cocked the pistol. "Plans can change. But the answer is no, because if it were a true statement it would presume she had any brains to start with. Sadly, she don't. Take a leap of faith, Rossington, like your father afore you."

Willoughby stood leaning into the wind, balanced on the edge of the cliff. He swallowed. The horror showing on Beth's desperate face touched him deeply, as fear and anger gripped his heart and soul. The shot that rang out nearly wrong footed him enough to go over the edge as the horse reared. Beth was thrown to the ground. Willoughby threw himself towards the land and rough grass. Spratt fought to regain control of the startled animal.

Willoughby sprang to his feet, never more grateful to feel solid earth below them and grabbed the reins with one hand and Spratt's sleeve with his other. Spratt hit Willoughby across the face with the pistol, striking his cheek hard; the horse bolted.

He glanced down and saw Beth was all right, although shaken and upset. Abner appeared along the coastal path with his rifle in hand. Willoughby wrenched the gun from him, reloaded it, took position, aimed and fired. As Spratt rode the horse away along the coastal path, Willoughby shot across the cove and winged him. He lost control of the animal and fell.

Willoughby ran with the wind behind him, Abner following on.

"He's mine, Willoughby," Abner shouted.

"Go back, get men. We'll take him to the gaol. He'll hang like his father. We shall not be murderers, we shall bring justice." If Abner replied, Willoughby could not hear him as he gained ground upon the fallen man. Spratt was running with a limp.

Willoughby saw Spratt hit the ground; he suspected the man was about to fire and he too dropped to the grass. The shot flew past him, wild and desperate. Willoughby was up and after Spratt in a trice. The man could not pick up speed. His leg was bleeding. Willoughby launched himself at Spratt and brought him down with one blow to his wound.

Spratt turned and tried to throw the pistol like a missile at Willoughby's already bruised head but missed. Willoughby grabbed hold of Spratt, dragging him by the collar of his coat to the edge of the headland. Here it was higher and cut further out to sea, beyond the sand of the bay. He forced the man's head over the edge. "Look, you bastard! Look! This is what you sent my father to."

Spratt croaked, cleared his throat, spat blood and then managed to utter a few words. "Aye, but you ain't man enough to do it. You have a conscience ... you is weak ... like a priest."

Willoughby was about to pull him back. Honour told him he must hand him to the assizes and see him hang at the end of a rope, giving justice and peace to all his victims, once and for all. But instead, it was he who was spun around and tossed aside like a piece of flotsam onto the shore. Abner held Spratt on tiptoe so that his wiry frame depended on the strength of Abner's arm for its survival.

Spratt's eyes were unnaturally wide. His sharp tongue failed him as he clung to Abner's arm.

Beth, breathless, appeared at Willoughby's side. "Don't, Abner. You're too good for that. Let him hang. Mr

Willoughby's right. Murder him in cold blood and you are as good or as bad as he."

Abner squeezed Spratt's neck in his large hand.

"Enough, Abner!" Willoughby said, and Abner, with a look of hatred mixed with disgust, nodded. He let Spratt drop to the grass on the edge of the path.

"Thank you ... mercy ... thank you..." Spratt's chant, hardly discernible, surprised them as he grovelled on the ground. For a moment they looked to each other puzzled, but Willoughby knew the man well enough. Spratt had misjudged him for the last time.

Abner took his eyes off Spratt to speak to Beth. The man sprang from the ground. He tried to launch himself at Abner and send him over the edge. Willoughby, with one deft swing of the rifle, doubled Spratt in two with the force of the blow. He staggered, holding his belly with his arms. His leg gave way. He stumbled backwards and both Abner and Beth stepped aside as the man fell headlong over the edge.

"Amen!" Abner said, as he stared down, crossed himself and picked up the pistol, taking the rifle from Willoughby's hand. Without further word he began walking slowly back towards the hall.

"Abner," Willoughby shouted.

The man stopped and looked over his shoulder back to them, with tired eyes.

"Miss Tully has sent word that she will arrive by the end of the month. She will be helping Elizabeth to adapt to her new life."

Abner nodded and continued to walk to the Hall, his head seemed higher and his stride more urgent.

Beth looked at Willoughby, slipping her hand into his. "It's over, Willoughby."

He squeezed her hand gently. "God's will, be done." He looked to the sea and then the sky. He had his answer; he would always have his faith, but he'd never wear the robes of a priest again. Willoughby stared down at the young woman next to him. "It's time for life to begin again for us, Elizabeth. Let us go home."

# A NOTE TO THE READER

Dear Reader,

Thank you for choosing to read *To Love, Honour and Obey*. I hope you found Willoughby's and Beth's adventure both enjoyable and satisfying. Below are some notes on the historical backdrop and the inspiration behind the story.

## The Early Nineteenth Century

The early nineteenth century was a period of great conflict and change: a time of war, pressgangs, extreme social, agricultural, religious and political changes. All these impacted on the ordinary people who were left behind, whilst the wars with Napoleon dragged on.

The government taxed its people harshly, whilst still fearing the possibility of a revolution as had happened in France. It was hardly surprising then that smuggling and opportunists abounded, yet in plying the trade they gave coin to an enemy. Some gangs were known for their violence, others were less so and merely supplied a ready market that crossed over social rank and was often funded by a moneyed man.

With the onset of the Industrial Revolution and the growth of new money, lives were changing and the old money was feeling threatened.

In the cities 'society' had strict rules: influence and connections were so important.

In my stories the settings are more remote. These influences mean nothing when a character is dealing with survival, either their own, or someone who they have met. So boundaries are crossed, rules of society are broken or are irrelevant. People who should never meet in the old order fall in love and carve out a new future.

## The Characters

Beth and Willoughby have something in common from the beginning. Beth was disadvantaged from birth: she was born a female in a very male orientated world. Her parents disowned her and so she was at the mercy of an uncaring system. Then she is sold into what could have been a very predictable path had fate not intervened. However, Beth is strong; she has a quick wit and a determined spirit and dares to dream. From the point at which Willoughby crosses her path, there is no looking or going back for her.

Willoughby is from an affluent family, so has comfort and food unlike Beth. However, his family have coerced him into following the life of a priest rather than that of a soldier. His uncle runs the estate whilst his elder brother was commissioned into the army. So Willoughby thinks he has no choice, but serves his King and Country fighting a clandestine war. His quest is his passion. Once the war is done then he will be free to choose his path.

They are two completely different characters, who both have their dreams, but who would never have met in Polite Society.

## The Region

Most of my titles are set in an area of the country that I love: North Yorkshire, with its beautiful coast and moors.

Set before Nelson's victory and untimely death at Trafalgar, Willoughby and Beth's adventure takes them from the beautiful city of York, with its majestic Minster towers, to the ancient whaling port of Whitby. The striking red-pantiled roofs, old abbey ruins and the church of St Mary on the headland, down to the working busy River Esk that the young James Cook was so familiar with, provide a colourful backdrop. I have taken the liberty of moving a temporary barracks of dragoons in for the period.

I also created an Alum working north of Whitby, based upon the Peak mine workings at Ravenscar. There were many such workings in the region where conditions were harsh for the ordinary man and woman.

From here they venture north to the rugged headland of Stangcliffe, the scene of the first murder and the beginning of Willoughby's quest. Anyone who has seen the aerial views taken in the TV docudrama The Mighty Redcar will have seen the sweeping sandy bay with Huntcliffe at one end, my Stanglciffe. Based on the Saltburn-by-Sea that shelters in its shadows, my Ebton was born, with its Coble Inn nestled on the beach.

Love is a timeless essential of life. Throughout history, love in all its forms is a constant: be it passionate, caring, needy, manipulative, possessive or one that is strong enough to cross barriers of culture or faith. When two souls meet in a situation which takes them out of their normal social strata or into a shared danger, a relationship forms as the adventure unfolds.

If you enjoyed reading *To Love, Honour and Obey* I would really appreciate it if you could take a moment to leave a review either on **Amazon** or **Goodreads**, or wherever you wish.

It is always helpful to read feedback and I am always interested in what my reader's think, or would like to read next.

I can be contacted on:- Facebook: **ValerieHolmesAuthor**, Twitter: **@ValerieHolmesUK**, or through my website: **www.ValerieHolmesAuthor.com**.

Love the Adventure!

**Sapere Books** is an exciting new publisher of brilliant fiction and popular history.

To find out more about our latest releases and our monthly bargain books visit our website: **saperebooks.com**

Printed in Great Britain
by Amazon